LYON'S PREY

The Lyon's Den Connected World

Anna St. Claire

ARE YOU SIGNED UP FOR DRAGONBLADE'S BLOG?

You'll get the latest news and information on exclusive giveaways, exclusive excerpts, coming releases, sales, free books, cover reveals and more.

Check out our complete list of authors, too!

No spam, no junk. That's a promise!

Sign Up Here

www.dragonbladepublishing.com

Dearest Reader;

Thank you for your support of a small press. At Dragonblade Publishing, we strive to bring you the highest quality Historical Romance from the some of the best authors in the business. Without your support, there is no 'us', so we sincerely hope you adore these stories and find some new favorite authors along the way.

Happy Reading!

CEO, Dragonblade Publishing

PROLOGUE

December 1815
Epsom, Surrey, England

WHAT IS TAKING *the miserable doctor so long?* Evan Prescott, the fifth Earl of Clarendon, poured another measure of brandy and took a long sip. The heartbreaking screaming coming from upstairs had gone on for hours. Rogue tears slid down his face as he stared at the open door to his study, and he brushed them aside. He wanted it to be over *for her.*

Evan had sent for her family and his, but the weather was making it difficult for anyone to get there. He only hoped the doctor would make it soon. The frosted glass of the large windows drew him, conflicting with the warmth of the room and the brandy. He rubbed some frost away with the side of the hand holding the brandy to peer outside. The pristine beauty of the snow and full moon offered a sharp contrast to the terror he felt inside. Heavy snow covered everything, leaving an almost fairy tale quality to the grounds glimmering beneath the moonlight. It had been snowing all day and showed no signs of letting up.

A throat cleared behind him, and he turned to see his butler, Bernard, standing near him.

"My lord, the doctor has arrived. His carriage got stuck in a snowdrift, and he had to leave it and walk the rest of the way. He is about the size of your father, so I ordered some dry clothes for him. Do you wish to speak with him before he goes upstairs?"

"Thank God! Thank you for getting him some warm clothes. My needs are all upstairs. Please send him to my wife at once."

A piercing scream rent the air, causing both men to jump.

"Immediately, please. She needs him now."

"Right away, my lord." The older man scrambled to move quickly but knew only one speed.

Unable to control his growing frustration, Evan walked to the door and stuck his head into the hall. "Good God, man. *Hurry.*" He immediately regretted his action, even though the sound of footsteps almost running away from his door felt more satisfying. Taking a deep breath, he walked to the fireplace and leaned against it, staring as the flames licked wood and ricocheted off the back of the chimney and into the night sky. Evan pressed the now warm glass of brandy to his forehead to dispatch a pounding headache, feeling a weakness he had never known before.

"God, please pull her through this," he said aloud to himself. While he was not deeply religious, Amelia was. "I promise to be a better man; please do not take my wife away." He swiped at the tears that ran down his face.

Thoughts flooded his mind. Amelia had pronounced the house ready for Christmastide, having been on her feet against his wishes, supervising the footmen and maids as they assembled boughs throughout the house. "It is snowing, and you know how I love it. Will you take me on a sleigh ride?" Amelia had pleaded. She wanted fresh air, tired from the bedrest of the past four months. They even joked about how they may not get another sleigh ride like this for a while after the baby came.

Rather than disappoint her, he ordered the sleigh and horses brought around, and the two took a ride into the village and purchased trinkets for the baby.

His wife wanted a little boy that looked like him, with dark brown hair and brown eyes. Evan wanted a girl, one that had rosy cheeks, blue eyes, and curly blonde hair like her mother. A son could come later, if that was what happened. He could cherish a house full of girls that all resembled their mother. His own mother was pushing for a son to carry on the family name, constantly reminding him of their duty to produce an heir. Amelia would gently respond that she would do her best. His wife understood his mother, something he struggled to comprehend, yet was always grateful for.

Memories clawed at him. The two of them had had the road to themselves that afternoon, laughing and kissing as they rode with the snow swirling around them. The clop-clop of the horses' hooves rhythmically hitting the earth created a romantic, memorable moment.

"This is the most wonderful day, Evan," Amelia enthused, snuggling closer under the blanket. "Tell me again that you will be all right if this turns out to be a girl instead of a boy."

Evan lightly touched her pert red nose with his forefinger. "Yes, darling. I love this child, whatever it may be. I mean that." He kissed her nose, basking in her smile.

They spent the afternoon discussing names again, cuddling together under the thick cover as the driver took them on roads, some with perfectly shaped canopies covered in fluffy snow crystals. It had been a day full of beauty and only the hundredth time they had discussed names in a fortnight. They both liked the name Jason, after his father. However, she liked Edward, saying it was a potent name, and as his second name, it was her favored choice. They decided if it was a girl, the baby would take Amelia's mother's name. By the time they returned, he realized that they had still made no decision on the boy's name, but it mattered not. They would meet the babe first.

Stark quiet invaded his thoughts. *How long has Dr. Pembroke been up there? It is too quiet.* Unable to wait another minute, Evan threw his drink into the fire and hurried from his office, taking the steps two at a time, praying. The thirsty wail of a baby caused him to stop and look up. *There are no voices.* He reached his wife's room in a trice and flung open the door.

Amelia's lifeless body lay on sheets still pooled with blood.

"My lord, she . . ." Her maid's tear-stained face saw him approaching, and she hurried away from the body to stand near the wall.

"No!" he howled, moving Amelia's hands to his shoulders and pulling her up to him as he cried into her damp blonde hair.

Dr. Pembroke put a hand on his shoulder, and he pushed it away. There was no comfort. He could have no life without Amelia.

A weak cry sounded behind him, and he tried to turn from Amelia to see the baby.

"My lord, you have a son," the midwife whispered brokenly, offering the small child to him.

Swiping at his face, he looked down at the bundle of wrinkled pink skin. Carefully laying his wife back down, he reached for the baby. Blue eyes framed by tiny wisps of blond hair looked into his face, and a small hand grabbed his finger and held on.

"Edward. You are Edward." He smoothed back the baby's hair as the door opened.

His sister had arrived. Through swollen eyes, he watched her glance first at Amelia, then at Edward before rushing to his side.

"Evan, oh my God! How... what can we do to help?" Catherine said tremulously, pressing her hands to her ashen cheeks.

"She is gone. My Amelia is gone," he cried hoarsely, thrusting the baby into her arms.

"Where are you going?" she screeched after him.

Evan stopped and half-turned to face his sister. "I need air," he croaked, looking down once more at the bed and noticing the rattle and cloth doll he and Amelia had purchased just that day. "Please understand."

I am broken.

CHAPTER ONE

December 1816
London, England

E VAN PRESCOTT PUSHED himself up from his mattress and squinted at the windows. The deep green velour curtains had been pulled back, allowing the bright morning sunshine to beam into his room—and straight into his face. "God's teeth, Charles! It is too early to get up," he groaned loudly. Irritated with his valet, he buried his head into his pillow, pounding on the mattress. A vague memory of Charles trying to yank off his boots while he slept pricked his senses. Except for his boots, he was still fully clothed. *There had better be a good reason for waking me at this ungodly hour.*

His head hurt *a lot*—testament to his almost nightly routine of brandy, cards, and more brandy. As long as he continued to hold a winning hand at the table, he saw no reason to quit, and he had no memory of losing the previous evening. His new routine kept him focused on the part of his life that he could control, the part that—outside of a resounding headache—did not hurt. He liked the cards because he was always a winner. He was *not* a winner in marriage.

Evan still felt numb from the loss of his wife. Amelia had died in childbirth. They had been betrothed by their parents. They had been neighbors, then playmates and lifelong friends, and finally man and wife. He had loved Amelia. His wife had died meeting her obligation to give him an heir. That was how he saw things now. He hated the word—*obligation*. He could not hide his feelings. He had hated his familial obligation and now he had another obligation, a *parental* obligation. Evan had a son and knew nothing about parenting. He had not even seen his son in months. His sister felt strongly that he needed to know his son, but Evan did not know how to fulfill that responsibility. He *could* hire someone, he supposed. He dared not think of Amelia and what she would say if she saw him today.

Charles had been part of his household as long as Evan could remember, having also served Evan's father, the former Earl of Clarendon. The man took more liberties than a valet should—or at least that was what his screaming head was impressing upon him after being subjected to the cruel morning sun. He should speak to Dean, his man of business, and secure a new valet. He *would* if these were better times. He would hire one that obeyed his wishes and did not foist his own opinions on his betters. "Devil it!"

Evan took a deep breath and rolled over, resolved to face the sun. *Who am I kidding? I only made it home from the club intact last night because Charles collected me.* No other valet would not have made it his business. Evan had been totally foxed and staggering in the alley when Charles had coaxed him into the coach. He vaguely recalled sitting against the dark velvet blue squabs of his carriage. He could have been robbed, killed, or worse had Charles not come for him.

"You have visitors, my lord," Charles's deep voice broke into his thoughts.

"This early? Tell them I am not available," Evan rasped.

"I took the liberty of accepting the message from Bernard for you, my lord." The valet drew a breath. "Your bath is already prepared. I do not believe either of these callers will easily be put off. I believe you should see them," Charles urged quietly.

"Really? *You* feel I should see them?" His voice dripped with sarcasm, and Evan lamented his tone at once. *God, my head hurts.* "Why do you think I should see them?" He tried to ask more plaintively.

"Because, my lord, Lord and Lady Rivers are here to see you, and they have Lord Edward." Charles hesitated. "And the other woman."

"There is another woman besides my sister?" Evan started.

"Yes, my lord. While I did not catch her name, the lady was quite emphatic that she should see you. She told Bernard that your carriage nearly killed her brother while they were shopping in Mayfair yesterday afternoon. I overheard her say she is not going away until she sees you," Charles responded evenly. "Your sister is with Lord Edward and Lord Rivers in the nursery and has requested you meet her there. Bernard placed the other visitor in the study and asked that tea be served."

"What the hell? Dammit!" Evan could not be mad at Charles. He was, however, mad at himself. He knew he had been drinking and gaming a fair amount. Perhaps he needed to . . . what, exactly? He had little memory of the day before. This had happened in Mayfair? Had he just left the house? Crikey! He could not even remember leaving. Had it happened on the way to the Lyon's Den? He had no memory from the gaming hell, except winning. He *always* won.

Guilt gripped his heart, a now-familiar feeling. Guilt was all he felt these days when he was not drinking. He needed to parent Edward. The baby would be a year old in a week, and Evan rarely had anything to do with him. His dead wife's face flashed in his mind, forcing Evan to squeeze his eyes closed. Her gut-wrenching screams were replaced by a single lusty cry from his son, but all else was silent. Amelia had died, and it was because of him. He had killed his own wife.

"No. Please inform Catherine that I have commitments. I will drop by to see them later in the day or tomorrow." Evan glared at Charles.

"Do you have something more?" Fatigue made it difficult to hold his temper.

"As you wish, my lord." Charles's mouth pinched tightly as he nodded and left to relay his employer's message.

"Charles, have my driver see me when my guests have departed."

"Yes, my lord." The valet inclined his head.

He watched his valet leave as he sat back on his bed, throwing his head against the headboard in exasperation. Evan had been a perfect ass. He knew it. He stared out of his bedroom window and suddenly felt trapped. No one cared what *he* wanted. He needed more sleep, but that was his own fault. Evan knew the women would still be waiting regardless of anything Charles told them. His sister was stubborn when she felt justice was on her side. And the other woman? He had a niggling feeling that she would not leave either.

What was wrong with him? He had two women waiting on his presence. Evan was no coward, but he dreaded the conversation he would have with his sister. Catherine had a purpose for being there, and he needed to see her first.

Charles had only been gone a few minutes. Grabbing his green velvet dressing gown, he secured it and walked to the door, opening it slightly. His housekeeper, Mrs. Hutchins, buzzed past with an armload of towels. "Mrs. Hutchins," he caught her attention.

"Yes, m'lord?" The elderly housekeeper stopped in the hall and turned to curtsy, almost losing all the folded towels.

He did his best to help her pick up the fallen towels without exposing himself. "I know your arms are full, but when you have a minute, could you let my sister know I will see her in the nursery in fifteen minutes, after all? And please alert Bernard that I will be down shortly afterward to see the lady waiting in my study. Make sure scones and fresh tea are served."

"Yes, m'lord." The elderly woman hastily bobbed a curtsy and scurried down the hall.

Evan eased himself into the now cold bathwater, rushing his toilette. He shivered, knowing Charles had probably ordered it warm, realizing it would be cold before he used it. Penance for his mischief last evening. Evan should be angry, but it would be a waste of his time and energy. Charles would not be changing, and he would not be firing him. Evan enjoyed fantasizing about it, but in truth, the man was indispensable and knew it.

A short time later, Evan stood quietly outside the door to the nursery and watched his sister coo over his young son by the window. The nursery looked much the same as it did when they had used it as children. Dust particles glittered through the morning beams of sunlight that shone through the window. The room needed a thorough cleaning.

The picture over the small bed he used to sleep in caught his attention. It had been a long time since he had seen this painting. His mother had painted it of his father and himself fishing with cane poles by the stream. Both had had their backs to his mother, so that was how she had painted it. He had forgotten that his father used to take him fishing. Once upon a time, they had been close, he and his father, going everywhere they could together—visiting tenants and friends in the surrounding areas, fishing, hunting.

His mother's artistic talent was phenomenal. She had also painted the small scene above his sister's bed that had his father, sister, and him in it. They were playing pall mall. The mallets were almost as tall as his sister. He recalled that day. Catherine had gotten frustrated with the balls not going where she wanted them. She dropped her mallet down and moved the balls through the hooped wicket with her hands, giggling with excitement as they rolled through.

When his father's health began to falter, his sire withdrew into himself, and most of these earlier memories were hidden behind more recent ones of contention and a constant stream of criticism. He could not please his sire no matter how he tried. He and Amelia had married after her first season to please Father, but that had not produced the desired results. The relationship between father and son had suffered so much neglect that nothing seemed to help. Still, this picture reminded him there had been a different life with his parents—one of happiness and laughter—instead of the distance and frustration that had seized his memories.

Can I be that kind of father to Edward? He knew in that moment that he wanted to try. He owed it to his son and Amelia. Evan needed to be a father to his child.

"Looking at you with Edward reminds me of Mother," he said softly as he walked up behind his sister.

"Evan, I did not hear you approach." Catherine turned slowly and kissed the baby's head before looking up at him. "He looks a lot like you. He is trying to walk already, you know." She put her nephew down, and he tried to toddle to a nearby toy, quickly dropping to all fours and crawling to it.

As if trying to show his father what he had learned, his son sat up and turned around, standing and toddling a few steps in his direction. Evan swallowed, fighting a sudden roiling in his stomach.

"Where is Tom?" he asked, suddenly uncomfortable. He glanced around the room, looking for his brother-in-law.

"Tom is behind me." She stepped aside and motioned toward the schoolroom side of the nursery where his brother-in-law leaned back in a rocker, reading a book from the small bookshelf of children's books.

"Tom, it is very good to see you." Evan walked toward his sister's husband, his hand extended.

"It is good to see you looking well." Tom shook his hand. "Although, we have been concerned."

A moment of silence ensued. Evan bristled. His brother-in-law had never been a man to mince words. They had taken care of Edward almost since the day he was born and, like it or not, he needed to allow for their opinions.

"Would you like to hold your son?" His sister looked at him with that expression she and Mother had perfected when vexed. It was a look of condemnation. He was glad his mother had gone on tour and was not home to add to his vexation. "You have not come by to check on him in weeks—and only a handful of times since his birth. Word is you are drinking and . . ." Catherine's ever-ready tears spilled from her eyes.

"You have been checking up on me?" He recoiled.

"I do not have to check up on you," she retorted, drawing up at the accusation in his tone. "You have been the subject of gossip and speculation. You were in *The Gazette* this morning. When do you plan to begin your parental duties? It has been a year since Amelia died."

"Easy, Catherine." Tom rested his arms on his wife's trembling shoulders.

Her blistering words threatened to turn Evan's earlier resolution to dust.

As if she could hear his thoughts, Catherine gently handed Edward to him.

Evan stared. *Fatherhood.* Impulsively, he held his son close, feeling his heartbeat and that of his son. Warmth washed over him. A whimper drew his attention down to the cherubic face staring up at him. "I cannot take him yet, Catherine . . ."

"Evan!"

"Hear me out. Give me until the end of this week. Five days." His own voice sounded foreign to him. "I promise. I will make things right for Edward." He was not sure what this entailed, but surely he could hire someone to handle things.

"Understand that I am not saying I do not love this boy—I do." She blinked back tears. "He is a wonderful baby." She looked at Tom, who indicated agreement with her. "Fine. Take the next few days and get your head together, brother. It is time for you to become his father in more than just name."

The nanny's room door opened, and a graying woman stepped out.

"Mrs. Donner. Your timing is perfect." Catherine turned to her brother. "Evan, Mrs. Donner is your son's nurse and has been a wonderful help with Edward."

This could be the answer to his prayers. He would hire a nanny—*maybe this nanny*—and take his time getting to know his son.

The older woman approached the small group. "My lords, if you would like, I can take the boy." She gestured, holding out her hands.

Evan glanced from his sister and brother-in-law to the nanny. "I understand you enjoy your services to my son. Lord and Lady Rivers are very complimentary of you, and I find I am in need of a nanny. I would very much appreciate it if you would join my staff at the end of the week." Was this him speaking? It was his voice. An hour before, he would not have guessed he would be taking on a small boy. *His* small boy.

"Thank you, my lord. The young lord is an agreeable child. He has a pleasing way about him that could pull a smile from the grumpiest of men. He is a happy child." She smiled. "I am happy to oblige."

My son is happy? He lost his mother, and his father has done nothing but ignore him. Yet he was happy. Evan noticed that just this short period with his son had lifted his mood. Perhaps having the boy there would be exactly the tonic he needed. Or it could cause him to *need* a tonic. He was not sure, but it appeared the decision was largely out of his hands.

"Mrs. Donner, I want to move Edward into his nursery, and your continued services will make things easier. My housekeeper, Mrs. Hutchins, plans to freshen the room. If you have a favorite color, please let her know, and we will endeavor to obtain it for you." It was a small price to pay for someone he was entrusting his son to. He smiled at his sister, who swiped at her eyes behind Mrs. Donner. *Jesus, she cries when she is mad, and she cries when she is happy.*

"Oh, Lord Clarendon, that is a wonderful offer. I should think a pale blue with hints of yellow would provide a bright and cheery background for the nursery. And if it pleases you, my lord, I am particularly partial to lavender. That would be such a nice color for my own room."

He had committed, and there was no turning back. *How on earth did I get to this moment when all I wanted to do was sleep this morning?* Shaking off the self-serving thoughts, he smiled. "I believe those small requests can be arranged." He handed his son to the nurse. "Thank you for your help, Mrs. Donner."

"You are welcome, my lord," she said, taking the child. She looked back at his sister and bobbed her head. "I will wait in the hall, my lady."

"Thank you, Mrs. Donner," Tom spoke up. "Catherine, we should let your brother get to his other guest."

Evan touched his sister's arm. She could make him angry, but he adored his sister. She turned, and he pulled her close. "I am truly sorry that I have put you and Tom in this position. I realize that Edward is my responsibility and I need to start being accountable for him. You have been—no, you *are* a wonderful sister. Thank you." He gave her a quick kiss on the forehead. "If you can excuse me, I have kept someone waiting in my study."

Catherine exhaled loudly and dipped her head. "We will be back later this week, Evan."

He watched his sister and brother-in-law leave once more with his son. This time, however, he felt a curious glimmer of hope.

Chapter Two

EVAN STOOD ON the second-floor veranda and watched his brother-in-law's black coach with a gold-encircled R emblem depart. Finally, he turned and headed toward his study. He could not seem to rid himself of the strange knot that had formed in his stomach and simply attributed it to tension. His body still suffered from lack of sleep, but his curiosity had awakened. Good grief! He wanted to sleep. However, a young woman had demanded to see him and had waited in his study nearly an hour. Bernard had told him she refused to leave before seeing him but showed herself very appreciative of the tea and biscuits.

He paused outside his study door before entering, fortifying himself and gathering his wits. He needed a moment after the emotional tussle he had just had with Catherine and Tom. *What is this about?*

Determined to address the woman's issue and send her packing, Evan opened the door and stopped. A red-headed woman wearing a black dress and a burgundy velour pelisse turned away from his picture window and stared at him through the greenest eyes he had ever seen. Her loose hair cascaded down her back in long spirals.

"My lord." Her words were curt as she bobbed her head, wearing a look of disgust.

"You have me at a clear disadvantage, my lady," he ventured, giving her an opportunity to provide her name and state her business.

"I apologize for this interruption to your day." She narrowed her emerald green eyes. "However, your carriage nearly ran down my brother Jason on St. James's Street yesterday, before eventually stopping at your club so you could obtain *nourishment*," she said, her tone dripping with anger and sarcasm. "He is but ten and pulled from my hand for a moment, thinking to run across to the flower vendor."

He blinked. The wisp of a woman standing in front of him had verbally attacked him as if he was an underling of hers. She clenched her small hands into fists at her sides, and her green eyes shot daggers at him.

"What did you say your name was and"—he glanced warily around the room—"did you bring a chaperone?" Honestly, he needed a drink. "It is not my custom to entertain ladies alone in my study."

She stammered. "I . . . I did not bring my chaperone with me this morning," she said haltingly, as if just realizing it herself. "I am Lady Charlotte Grisham. My younger brother is the Earl of Romney, and you *nearly* killed him. He is a child, and your carriage did not even stop!"

Evan struggled to process what she was saying. Something with the names seemed off. "Surely you have confused . . ." Her back stiffened, causing him pause. He took a deep breath. "I apologize for my poor choice of words. May we begin again?"

She nodded.

"Lady Charlotte, I do not recall seeing you or your family carriage. I am familiar with the crest." Realization hit him. "My God! I do know of your family. My sincerest condolences on the loss of your father." His mother had made known to him her friendship with Lady Romney and had paid her a visit shortly before she left the country. "I know your older brother, Matthew—Lord Longueville. I will speak with him and offer . . ." The pained look on her face made him stop. "My lady? Did you say your *younger* brother was the Earl of Romney?" Matt had shared some of the details of his difficult relationship with his father. When they had finished school, he had enlisted in the military and left for what seemed like a friendly enough post in America. Was it the army or the navy? He could not recall. They had all been good friends in school, but no one had heard from Matt in several years. "Has something happened to Lord Matthew?" His voice rasped as he intoned his friend's name.

She gripped the back of the chair that stood in front of his desk and looked at him with shimmering eyes. "My brother has not been heard from in over a year. He was lost in the Battle of New Orleans." Her voice trembled. "With the death of Papa, my younger brother has been declared the heir."

"I am sorry. I do not recall your brother or anyone darting in front of my carriage, but I intend to speak with my driver right away about the incident," he said with concern. "However, that does not mean I do not believe it happened." In softer tones, he continued. "Your younger brother, Jason—how is he? I mean, is he all right?" He had awoken to a day full of nightmares. Perhaps it was some weird day of reckoning. Three hours before, he had been lost to sleep and dreams. Just three hours.

"Surely you are not saying that you had no idea you were traveling at a higher rate of speed than was safe. Considering where you were heading, perhaps you were already *foxed!*" She regarded him with a look of total disgust.

"You forget yourself, *my lady*. I admit to no such thing, and you go too far to cast aspersions on my behavior. I said I would speak to my *driver*. I did not see your brother myself." Evan's jaw tightened. Truth be told, he had been more than slightly inebriated, but the woman went too far. Even so, a wave of guilt beset him.

"I do not understand how you missed him. Your driver never even slowed. If Matthew were here . . ." She paused. "A respectable person would not have driven at that speed on that road."

"You overstep *again*, my lady," Evan's temper flared. "You continue to rebuke me for something I did not do. I *informed* you I will speak to my driver."

"I do nothing of the sort, my lord. I am simply repeating for understanding. My brother was almost cut down by your carriage. Had I not seen the carriage's path soon enough and grabbed him, he could have been killed. As it was, *your carriage* barely missed the two of us." Her voice oozed disdain. "*You*, my lord, kept going and stopped down the road at a house known for its lascivious conduct. I thought to make you aware of the seriousness of your behavior. We both fell trying to get out of the way. A gentleman stopped for us and recognized your carriage. He helped us into our conveyance after ascertaining we had only a few scratches. Perhaps it was borne of foolishness, however we thought something was wrong, so my driver pursued you in our carriage until you arrived at your *destination*." She spat the last word at him, her distaste evident. "I decided to confront you here, rather than *there*."

Her words pierced him and fed his anger. What? Who stopped? *They had followed him?* He wanted to ask more but bit his tongue. Evan's driver had almost cut down a peer and a lady—with him in the carriage. A display of temper would most likely cause even more trouble. "May I ask where exactly this happened?"

"As a matter of fact, it was just a few streets from here, near Grosvenor Square," she replied.

That was the route he usually followed to the Lyon's Den. Had his driver nearly run the boy over without his realizing it? Impossible, surely. He could not even recall the ride to the club. Not recalling anything was as upsetting to him as what he had been accused of doing, making it impossible for him to deny. What had he become in his grief?

"Your brother, *he is unhurt*? And you . . . ?" He clenched and unclenched his fists, remorseful and unnerved by his own behavior. "I am sorry for my lapse. You must let me make this up to you."

Evan's concentration wavered as he tried to think about the incident, taking in the beauty berating him at the same time. He quietly eyed the tantalizing woman in front of him, silhouetted by the sun beaming though the window behind her. The sight of her chipped away at his preference for more generously curved women. He suddenly wondered how she might feel next to him, and this generated an immediate response from his own body. Guilt assailed him.

"*Making it up* would start with an apology, my lord," she replied in a milder tone.

"I have apologized," he rejoined tersely, suddenly frustrated at both his traitorous body and her question. He walked behind his desk and pulled a cord. "Let me prove my sincerity. I would like to meet Jason to see that he is unharmed." When Bernard arrived, he addressed him, "Have my carriage prepared at once. And ask for one of the reserve drivers."

"Yes, my lord. Right away." The tall, graying retainer nodded and backed from the room. The door clicked closed behind him.

"You want to come to my home?"

"That would be the general idea. Is there an objection? You have accused me of an unholy mistake on my part. I would like to ensure that no harm has come to your brother. I see it as a duty to Matthew as much as you."

"You presume too—" She stopped herself. "How do you know my brother Matthew? You act like there was a friendship . . ."

"Yes." He cut her off. "I do know your brother, or rather . . ." He paused. "Let us keep it at I know your brother. He could still be alive. Let us hope for that. Matt was a friend of mine at Eton—part of a group of friends, a foursome, that made school bearable." Evan could not resist the smile that swept over his face at the memory.

She tilted her head up and smiled, disarming him.

She is beautiful. How had he forgotten Matthew had a sister? He used to speak of her frequently.

"Yes, my brother would write me and tell me of some of the antics he and a group of boys played together. I believe he was fifteen at the time, maybe older. I am not sure if he mentioned you, but now I find myself curious enough that I must revisit his letters."

Her words tugged at his heart. "I am truly sorry for your family's losses and my driver's contribution to your angst. Has anyone gone to America to look for him?"

"My father talked about it, but I have heard nothing further. And now with father gone . . . My mother and I have met with his solicitor, and according to him, Father left no word as to whom he had engaged." A tear escaped the corner of her eye, and she quickly wiped it away. "Father . . . my mother and I, we must be mindful of our expenses. However, if there was any way possible that I could find my brother, I would."

"Tsk. If you will allow me to look into this for you and your mother, I would consider it a small way—a very small way—to make up for yesterday. Of course, had you or your brother been injured, nothing I could do would make up for such an accident." Truly, he still could not recall a thing about it. He would question his driver. He judged her to be telling the truth, and no matter what, he owed this. He had a hard time imagining his driver almost hitting a boy, but not remembering the episode was entirely plausible based on his conduct of late. He squinted. "My lady, if you will pardon my manners, I would consider it a favor if you could allow me to engage an investigator. I know just the man, and he has done this for at least one other family who had a son go missing. He is familiar with the hostilities in America and has availed himself of the . . . er . . . customs. I trust his work. I do warn that it could take some time to accomplish this." Sinclair was actually his friend Banbury's acquaintance, but she need not know that.

"You know of such a man? I have no words. My mother will be

overjoyed to have some sliver of hope that Matthew could be found alive. She has not been herself since Father's illness took him. Jason needs Mama."

How could he not help? The woman had mesmerized him, first chastising him fiercely, then proving to be the sister of his old friend. He would contact some of the others from their group and see who they knew of influence in the British Army.

"Then we shall provide her hope. Matt was a friend of mine. He would want his friends to help his family. I am afraid he lost touch with us not too long after school." He spoke but could not take his eyes off her. Her red hair was unlike most—a shade of burnished red with threads of honeyed blonde running through it. She was a remarkable beauty. Within a quarter of an hour, her face had moved from a look of total disgust to the most expansive and engaging smile he could remember. Evan wanted to know more about her, but first he needed to find her brother.

"Please do not take this the wrong way, but do you *feel* your brother is gone?" He watched Lady Charlotte Grisham closely as he asked. He believed that people possessed a certain level of sensitivity when it came to people they loved. What a strange twist this conversation had taken. He was actually relieved.

"My lord, you confuse me." She nibbled her bottom lip. "Actually," she said after a moment passed, "I do not believe my brother is dead. I think he is lost. I cannot shake the feeling that something has happened and he cannot find his way to us. But it is a curious question you ask. I believe my father felt the same way. He did not accept the loss. It was only after he died that my brother's title was conveyed. My uncle insisted."

"Your uncle?"

"Yes, Baron Langdale. He is my mother's brother. He petitioned to become my brother's guardian. Of course, my mother controls his daily activities, but her brother is now handling the financial affairs for the family." She glanced to the floor before looking back at him.

Evan discerned discomfort when she spoke of her uncle. Something felt amiss about this business, yet he was limited in his ability to do anything about it. "I know of the man." He held her gaze. "With your permission, I will find out what I can about your brother. Of course, if your brother is alive, I will do my best to return him, and you and your mother will no longer need the services of your uncle."

"Lord Clarendon, thank you. I do not know how this came to pass. I fear you have turned the tables on me. I stormed in here this morning to give you a piece of my mind, casting good sense to the wind. Yet I find myself encouraged with my anger stripped bare. And I feel we have both gained from our meeting."

"May I see you home? I did not notice a carriage outside."

"That is not necessary, my lord. I only live a few blocks from here . . ."

"My carriage is already waiting at the front door. If you will not allow me to accompany you, please allow my driver to take you home."

She drew in a breath. "That might be better. As you pointed out, I did not bring my maid. It is but a few blocks, but the weather does threaten a chilling rain." She caught his gaze. "Thank you."

Ten minutes later, Evan stood on the veranda and watched his carriage pull away with a most perplexing guest.

WHAT JUST HAPPENED? Lady Charlotte adjusted herself, pushing back into the squabs of the seat of Lord Clarendon's carriage. She tried to calm herself and account for the last hour. *For a man reported to drink all the time, Lord Clarendon had his wits about him. Today, at least. I suppose there is a chance that I have it wrong.*

She gave a wry laugh. Charlotte would have much to answer for if her mother saw her arrive in this carriage. Walking would have been better, except it was so cold outside. She took her gloved hand and rubbed the frost from the window, noticing for the first time that a layer of ice still covered many trees. When she had walked to the earl's townhouse earlier that morning, she was still angry over what had almost happened to her younger brother.

Lord Clarendon had seemed genuinely remorseful for his behavior, which had surprised her. Charlotte had been aware of the death of his wife in childbirth, but until today, she had not paid enough attention to the rumors about his son. She noticed the boy leaving with the nanny and Lord Clarendon's sister and her husband. The young lord was adorable. She grinned. He reminded her of her own little brother, Jason—the one the earl's carriage had almost run over yesterday. "Somehow, he turned the tables on me," Charlotte muttered. Jason was all she and Mama had now, and she would do anything to protect her baby brother. She should be frustrated but felt unusually charmed and hopeful.

Any chance of finding Matthew had seemed to have died with Papa. But now Lord Clarendon planned to help find her older brother, something that could not only heal her heart, but rid her family of her uncle's *helping* hand.

The carriage slowed to turn onto her street, and Charlotte smelled fresh pastries and other delightful smells coming from the corner bakery. Her family house was near. Inhaling deeply, she tried to still the racing of her heart. If she could just make it past the parlor where her mother normally sat watching the window . . .

CHAPTER THREE

E VAN COULD NOT remember when a dressing down had last been
so alluring, allowing for the fact that he had been made aware of
his poor behavior twice that day. That had to change. He knew that
and still found himself craving a drink. Hearing a horse pounding up
the drive, he looked past the carriage. Good God! Surely not another
onslaught. He squinted. It was his best friend, Lord Christopher
Anglesey, Earl of Banbury. His timing was impeccable. *Thank goodness!*
Evan craved a drink, and he would need Banbury if they were to have
a chance at finding Matt. He pulled on the cord, and a footman
appeared.

"Yes, my lord?"

"Ah yes. Stanton. Would you have Cook supply a tray of sandwiches, meats, and cheeses to my study? It seems I have another guest.
And two clean glasses, please. One more thing," he added as the
footman turned to leave. "Please have Bernard show my guest to the
study. And have some hot tea brought in—with peppermint. My
stomach feels a bit displaced."

"Right away, my lord." The tall blond footman left quickly.

Maybe Banbury can help make sense of my morning. Lady Charlotte mentioned someone helped her yesterday. His faith that the day could be salvaged suddenly renewed, he hurried toward his study. Voices in the anteroom behind him caused Evan to turn, and he saw his friend had arrived.

"Banbury, you are a sight for tired eyes this morning!" Evan walked toward his friend, extending his hand.

"Good to see you as well," Banbury smiled and clapped Evan on the back.

"Come in." Evan held open the door to his study. "I have already ordered luncheon."

"Wonderful. I am famished. By the way, who was that leaving in your coach?" Banbury turned around for emphasis and pointed toward the door. "I saw it and thought to have missed you. I was prepared to leave a message with Bernard."

"That is part of what I need to speak with you about. Ah, Stanton has arrived with our food. Come, let us take some refreshment."

The footman replaced the earlier tea tray with a fresh tray plated with meats, cheeses, and small finger sandwiches. "Can I be of any further service, my lord?"

"No, thank you, Stanton." Evan handed Banbury a plate, nodding at the food. "If you do not mind, there is something I would like to discuss."

"You have tea on that tray. Is there something you would like to tell me?" Banbury rose and gave a mock feel of his friend's head. "No fever."

Evan pushed his hand away. "All right, already! I have realized that I have allowed my depressed mood to debase my entire being and I am trying . . . to get hold, regain who I need to be." He grew quiet for a moment before pouring Banbury a cup of tea. "I hope you do not mind the peppermint. I have a bit of dyspepsia from yesterday's activities."

"I enjoy peppermint tea as well, but not for the same reason, I fear." Banbury snorted a laugh. "You outdid yourself yesterday, my good friend. We have much to discuss."

A frisson of cold traveled down his back. He had almost killed a young lad, wanted to fire his valet because the good man had done his job—more than his job—and he had neglected a son that he had not even taken the time to know. Not to mention a woman had bested him in an argument that morning. *No, it is already afternoon.* Christ, when did he start getting up at lunchtime? "I am aware that my behavior has been a bit off, but I endeavor to work on that."

Banbury nearly choked on his tea, spewing it all over himself. "*Off,* you call it?" His voice was incredulous. "Evan, I think my friend from a year ago would call it 'dipping rather deep.'"

"Yes, well, I am duly chastised. I want to be my old self." He quieted. "I just do not know how. Perhaps drinking tea instead of my customary brandy will help, but I confess, I would prefer the brandy."

"I understand." Banbury nodded. "Perhaps we should start with what you were wanting to talk to me about."

"It has to do with a woman." Evan glanced at Banbury, who had raised a brow. "Nothing like that," he quickly added. *Although she is a pretty sort*, he thought and immediately succumbed to guilt. "Do you know of a Lady Charlotte Grisham?"

"The Earl of Romney's daughter?" Banbury sat up. "She is a beautiful woman, but she is an innocent." His voice raised. "You surely have not ruined her, Evan?" His voice was filled with disgust.

"Good heavens, no! I have become a drunk, not a debaucher of innocents!" He deserved Banbury's scolding, he supposed. But coming from his best friend, who knew him better than anyone in the world, hurt. "I need to help her, and *no*," he emphasized. "I only met her this morning."

"I think you met her yesterday," Banbury corrected. "Your . . . er . . . *meeting* is part of what brings me here today."

"So it is true." He sank down in his chair and put his face in his hands. "I nearly killed her brother with my carriage, and I do not recall a thing."

"You did. I was not far behind you. We had been playing cards here, and you decided you needed a drink, and nothing would do but a trip to the Den. I was unable to dissuade you from going, so I spoke with Charles, asking him to return later with the carriage and collect you so you would not amble about the streets, as you have before."

"*You* told her my name?

"Me? No, of course not. But you were recognized by another, and I believe he blurted out your name in a string of curses. I stopped to make sure no one had been injured. *God's teeth, man!* The woman launched herself in front of your carriage to save her young brother. Both were injured, but miraculously, not seriously. And your carriage never slowed."

Evan grew quiet. It was all true, and the worst kind of truth. *I feel like a monster.* "I intend to speak with my driver, realizing that I too bear responsibility." He picked up his teacup, then set it back down without taking a sip. "I may as well ask my favor. It has to do with Lady Charlotte. Remember Longueville?"

"Yes, of course. It has been a while, but we had some great times with Matt. I did not make the connection when you first mentioned her name. He is in service now—the army, I believe."

"He is missing and has been for about a year, since the Battle of New Orleans. It was the last time anyone heard from him. According to Lady Charlotte, Matthew was also declared dead when the earl recently passed, prompted by her uncle. Her mother's brother has become the guardian and is in control of the finances. Do you know of Baron Langdale?"

There was a long moment of silence before Banbury finally spoke. "Yes, I know him." He exhaled with exaggeration. "That is not a good arrangement. As you know, he owes nearly everyone in town. How was it he was made guardian? Did no responsible party look into his affairs? Matt would want us to help. What can I do?"

"According to the lady, her uncle *insisted* on her brother being named the heir, and I think we both know why that happened. He still has friends in high places, unless he owes them too." He laughed sarcastically. "It may be easier to find Matt than to rid the family of the uncle's guardianship. But we should try both. Perhaps you can ask Sinclair? I believe he would be willing to do it, but more so if the request came from you. I do not know him as well, but I know he located two other men for their families when they had been declared missing. He is like a bloodhound."

"I will ask. Baron Langdale is known to raise a breeze or two for his own benefit. Her father was quite wealthy and made some shrewd investments, and this is quite a coup for him. The baron would not think twice about hanging on the sleeves of his nephew under the guise of guardianship."

"I will cover all expenses," Evan added.

"You know, it would be easier if she were married . . ." Banbury leaned back and grinned.

"Stop." Evan's tone was sharp. "I am sorry. I know you mean well, yet I urge you to quit this line of conversation. I am not ready to marry again." Nevertheless, he wondered. Perhaps obtaining a wife would help with a son. It could be a wise thing to do.

No. He could not lose another wife in childbirth. He *would* not.

"I may never be able to marry again. To lose . . ." His voice dropped off.

"I understand, Clarendon. I will help on both fronts. Has anyone tried to find her brother before this?" Banbury stood and walked to the window.

"According to Lady Charlotte, her father told her he had engaged someone to look for her brother, but she has no idea whom, and they never received any word on it."

"Romney and I use the same solicitor. Let me speak with Franklin and see what he knows. If Romney hired someone, it was probably through him." There was a moment of silence. "The Widow wishes to see you," Banbury inserted.

"Excuse me? What *widow* are we talking about?" Evan questioned, confused and frustrated.

"The Lyon's Den . . . the Black Widow has requested your presence."

He laughed. "You have to be bamboozling me! Too many people are requesting my presence today. My sister and brother-in-law have given me until Friday to take over the care of my son, and Lady Charlotte would not leave until she had an audience with me. And you, you are bringing the message from the Widow?" He eyed his friend with curiosity.

"I promise. 'Tis true. That is one reason I am here. Mrs. Dove-Lyon has asked to see you. For reasons only she can address, she sent word to me. One of her managers, a man named Luke Cross—he goes by the name Titan—witnessed your near accident yesterday. He recognized you, and now she wants to see you."

Evan had only ever seen the woman wearing black and veils. No one knew what her face looked like. Word was she kept a very close watch on her business. "Do you find it unusual that she has asked to see me?"

"I do. I should add, she has asked to see you *soon*."

Evan's resolve to leave off the brandy ended, and he grabbed two clean glasses from the cabinet in the corner of his office. Pouring a measure of refreshment into each, he handed one to his friend and took a long drink from his own.

"Do you think you should start that today?" Banbury ventured.

"Do *not* judge me," Evan snapped. "I know that I have been on the cut and spent more time in my cups this year than out of them. Nevertheless, I do not plan to become foxed. I still have a measure of control. And I do intend to enjoy a fortifying glass." He took a slow sip while his body demanded more. Whilst he had only been a member for a year, he had heard no good ever came from having to see the Widow.

Chapter Four

"THAT WAS THE Earl of Clarendon's carriage that just pulled away. I recognize the emblem on the front. Why is he dropping you off? Unchaperoned, no less!" Charlotte's mother hissed as she pulled her head from the window and looked at her daughter. "What were you up to, Charlotte?" she asked, arms crossed.

Mama spent all day, every day in this room. Charlotte stared at the pink room, looking for something on which to focus her attention. Her mother had insisted that the pink color in the room made the small room look larger than when it had been green. She had added a little yellow with the small pink and yellow floral drapes, but everything else was pink—walls, upholstery, carpet. For Charlotte's tastes, it was not comfortable enough to spend all day there. She consistently failed to interest Mama in any outing, picnic—anything.

Charlotte nibbled her lower lip, unsure of how much to say to her mother. "It was the Clarendon carriage. I had been to see him." She reminded herself that she wanted to look at her brother's letters. She was most curious about the man now that she had met him.

"Why did you go by yourself?" Her mother fairly shrieked the words before lowering her voice. "Beyond the fact that you could be ruined without a chaperone, you know his reputation of late. And your uncle—"

"Uncle does not have to know, Mama," Charlotte insisted. "Please let us keep this between the two of us."

Her mother's eyes watered, and she stiffened her shoulders. Charlotte prepared herself.

"Young lady, I do not know when you became so uppity, but I am your mother and deserve your respect. You would never act thus if your father was still here. Even so, you could make a worse match." Her mother sniffed.

"I apologize, Mama. Of course you are right. I should not have snapped. I am afraid I acted impulsively," Charlotte continued, "but Uncle does not need to know." She had lost quite a lot of respect for her uncle in the months that had followed Papa's death. She and Mama had gone from a life of ease while her father was around to one where every farthing was checked and accounted for with her uncle.

"I had purpose to my meeting, Mama. Lord Clarendon's horse nearly ran me over yesterday in Mayfair, and I gave him a piece of my mind. His sister and brother-in-law were there, so I was not alone." It was a stretch, but not really a lie. His family had pulled up when she arrived and left only a short while before she did. "Surely Lord and Lady Rivers qualify as adequate chaperones," she pressed. No way would she volunteer any information about her brother because that would put her mother over the top. Each day since Papa's death, her mother had eaten and dressed, but only sat in her parlor staring out the window. She barely paid attention to anything, and quite startled Charlotte with her observation of the carriage.

"Oh darling, you should mind your cheekiness in public. You know how your father felt about the sharpness of your tongue."

Her father would not have been happy.

"Certainly they would qualify as chaperones. The Dowager Clarendon and I are friends, you know." She looked at her daughter. "And no, I do not feel like speaking with my brother. He is always in such an ill temper of late." Her mother stopped. "He does not listen to what I have to say and says the harshest things to me. Your Papa . . ." Her voice trailed off.

Charlotte waited, careful not to cut her mother off again. She had never seen her mother as distraught as she had been since Papa's death. "Mama, I cannot help but wonder why we are not able to buy new clothes. Uncle limited us to two dresses each to observe Papa's mourning period. I had Jane dye some of my lighter dresses black so I would have a few more changes." She paused and took a calming breath before she continued. "Was Papa . . . are we without funds?" She swallowed. Charlotte had never worried about her clothing purchases before, yet her uncle was being very specific when it came to how much she and her mother were allowed to spend. Not only that, but her uncle was always telling her mother she had been spoiled and they needed to save money. Papa had cherished her mother.

"Your father always told me we would be well taken care of should something happen, so I do not understand why we are limited in our mourning attire—in everything, in fact. Even the household accounts are challenged. Dear daughter, I do not know what to think. My brother says we are quite *strapped*." The countess drew out the word in a huff.

It seemed her mother was beginning to question her brother. Still, Charlotte could not take the chance that Mama would see things as she did. At one and twenty years old, she was nearly firmly on the shelf. Had her father not passed and her brother not gone missing, she felt sure her life would have been different. However, it was to be the way of it, and she needed to accept things. Her uncle had made mention that it was high time she married. That, and the close attention he paid when she was near, was beginning to make her nervous. If they were as without funds as he claimed, perhaps she should consider employment. She worried so about her brother and mother. If her mother was more herself, she might consider it.

"My dear, I have sent word and asked to see a friend of mine to-morrow. I would like you to go with me," her mother said in a detached voice.

"You were out? I would have accompanied you wherever you needed to go today. It has been an age since we have gone anywhere together," Charlotte said solicitously.

"It truly has, my dear. But this was something I felt compelled to do, and when we are sure that we are alone, I will speak with you further. For now, please do not mention this to anyone."

Footsteps outside the door caused them to stop talking. A moment later, Mrs. Graves, the housekeeper, stepped inside. "My lady, your brother has arrived and has alerted Myers that a visitor is expected."

"Oh? Did he happen to mention who was expected?" Her mother inquired nonchalantly.

"I do not believe he gave the name, your ladyship," Mrs. Graves responded.

"If you happen to hear, I would be interested in quietly knowing," her mother's voice was almost a low whisper.

"Yes, my lady." The housekeeper gave a polite curtsey and left them alone. As if they were wary of her uncle themselves, the household—especially Myers, their butler, and Mrs. Graves—had become protective since Papa died. As with Mrs. Graves, they found ways to apprise them of her uncle's arrivals. How was it, though, that not even her lady's maid had mentioned Mama's outing to Charlotte? *Perhaps it was because you have been out yourself these two days past*, a voice in her head reminded her.

Mama had not been taking visitors—none that she had noticed, anyway. The only visitor was her uncle, and he came unannounced and had begun to use Papa's study as his own. Her blood simmered when she thought about it for reasons she could not quite understand.

While her uncle mostly annoyed her, her mother's activities took

Charlotte by surprise. Mama had behaved so despondently since Papa died, Charlotte would have never imagined she would leave their home at all, much less without her. *Just what is mother up to?* If she worried about it, it would just frustrate her, so Charlotte resigned herself to being content and busy for the rest of the day. She would find out soon enough.

The next morning her mother sent her maid up to ready her for a visit. Jane laid out her long-sleeved lavender-grey day dress and matching shoes, which Mama had approved. It was slightly better than the black or plain grey tones, *barely*. Once Charlotte dressed, Jane created soft curls to frame several loosely woven braids fashioned into a chignon. Turning side to side, Charlotte admired Jane's handiwork with a hand mirror. "You have never done this particular style. I like it." She smiled at her maid, eliciting a soft giggle.

"Thank you, m'lady. 'Tis something I saw on the fashion plates in the store when we were there last. I wanted to try it and am glad it pleases you."

Charlotte nodded and held up her mirror for one more peek. Noting the need for a bit of color, she pinched her cheeks. Satisfied with her appearance, she placed the looking glass down on her vanity and stood. "I am as ready as I will ever be. You have no idea who we are visiting today, do you?"

"No, m'lady. Your mother took a short visit somewhere yesterday, but I never thought to ask."

Mama is being very mysterious, she thought to herself as she made her way to the entry. There, she found her mother waiting.

"Put on your coat, dear. We have an appointment," her mother said, making her way out the door. "I would like to be home before your uncle visits. This is important." She scurried down the front steps to their waiting carriage.

The footman placed a small wooden block under the carriage door and handed both ladies up inside, where warm bricks awaited them.

That was thoughtful, she reflected, considering the weather was cold, and overcast skies threatened rain. "Mama, where did you say we are going?" Charlotte asked politely.

"I did not say, child, but we are going to see a woman who has agreed to help us."

"Help us? With what? I do not understand."

"Charlotte, you are one and twenty years of age. While your father and I would have supported additional seasons for you, we no longer have that luxury. I do not want you to suffer because you have no prospects. Added to that, we are in mourning for your dear papa, and my brother . . ." She stalled. "With the control that my brother is exacting, I am worried for you," her mother explained in a slow voice, one she used when she brooked little to no disagreement.

"I have not met the right man, Mama. Please tell me you are not doing something rash," Charlotte responded.

"No, I have not. However, your uncle has. I heard him speaking with a man of your father's years about wedding you. I heard no offer, but your uncle said . . . things." Her mother's head shook back and forth as if she was trying to deny to herself what she had heard. "I must protect my children."

"Mama, perhaps you misunderstood—"

"No, child." Her mother cut her off. "I know my own brother, and his heart is not always in control of his actions. Sometimes he is ruled by other . . . emotions."

That was a nice way to say her uncle was greedy. That was how she had heard her father describe him. *Why did Papa not make better arrangements for us in the event of his death?* They were pinching every bit of money they could, while she had noticed her uncle wearing much grander clothing. *I must stop this.* Thinking these thoughts about her uncle would only cause things to get worse.

The carriage pulled up in front of a nondescript blue building on Cleveland Avenue. Charlotte puzzled about it, as it was the same establishment she had seen Lord Clarendon enter after nearly hitting her brother. They were led to a side entrance and up the stairs to await the proprietress in a parlor completely decorated in red—red velvet curtains, a red velvet settee with carved gold arms, and red velvet armchairs. It was garish by any description. She recognized the large man outside as the man who had assisted them after Lord Clarendon's carriage had nearly run them down. Was there some connection? Did Mama know what had happened? A cold chill shot to her toes and she shuddered.

"Are you all right, my dear?" her mother tutted.

"I may or may not feel well," she hedged. "I think it may depend on why we are here," she added honestly.

"Do not be difficult, Charlotte. It is not like you," her mother said as she sat in one of the armchairs. Pale red wallpaper featuring a golden cherub pattern covered the walls, and a large crystal chandelier that might have been better suited to a large dining room hung above them.

Charlotte's hands suddenly felt frozen despite her gloves and muff. Nerves. Mama carefully looked in every direction except Charlotte's. She noticed her mother wiping a tear from the corner of her eye. Whatever was about to happen, Charlotte felt sure she was not going to be happy with it.

Moments later, a woman dressed head-to-toe in black, including a black veil that covered her face, swished into the room. "My dear Lady Romney. I hope I did not make you wait overlong. I had a small situation to handle."

"No, we only just arrived. Charlotte, this is Mrs. Dove-Lyon. Her husband was a friend of your papa's, and we have been acquainted a number of years." She turned to Mrs. Dove-Lyon. "This is my daughter, Charlotte."

"Ah! She *is* a beauty as you described." The proprietress sat down on her settee and began serving them tea. "I find orange tea to be the most refreshing, and with the season upon us, its blend is very satisfying."

Charlotte wondered whether orange was the only tea the woman drank. She sipped her tea and looked up, only to notice the woman eyeing her critically.

"I have given quite a bit of thought to your predicament," she started.

"What *predicament* are we talking about, exactly?" Charlotte asked, more and more fearful about this meeting.

Her mother set down her cup and looked at her sharply. "Charlotte, let us hear Mrs. Dove-Lyon out before you pepper her with questions."

"Yes, Mama." Her own reply was short, staccato-like.

"Lady Romney, I think she should understand why we are doing this. In order for it to succeed, she needs to participate," Mrs. Dove-Lyon corrected gently.

"You are right, of course," Mama responded, looking a little embarrassed. "Charlotte, while you are twenty-one years of age, your father's death has placed us in a situation. Your uncle still has tremendous influence over your future. I am concerned because while he thought I was sitting listlessly in the parlor, I was outside your Papa's study and heard him talking to a man I do not even know about marrying you off. When the man left, I saw that he was quite a bit older than you. While your Papa and I always wanted a love match for you, we never anticipated this type of thing could happen. I do not believe the bargain has been struck as of yet, and I sought out Mrs. Dove-Lyon for her counsel."

"I do not understand." Charlotte bit her bottom lip to keep it from trembling.

"Child, we need to move you out of your uncle's reach, or your life will take a turn you may not want," Mrs. Dove-Lyon interjected. "Now, we realize that we are 'arranging' this interlude, however, it is for your own good. I assure you, Lady Charlotte, I am only taking into account the best possibilities. I would like to give you a choice."

"Excuse me for sounding ungrateful, but it seems I am having my choice taken away from me," Charlotte fairly snapped.

Mrs. Dove-Lyon glanced at her mother and then to her. "I see that I may need to give you some other reasons. Yesterday, you were observed in the household of Lord Clarendon without your chaperone. Word has already reached my ears. I will not say how. But that will ruin you with the *ton*. Not only that, but you are in mourning, dear lady."

"I made a mistake. Surely, I can explain that away . . ." Charlotte saw the pained look on her mother's face and stopped talking.

"Daughter, your uncle plans to marry you off to Lord Thomas Butler. I asked Mrs. Graves to tell me who the visitor was. As I said, I do not know him. However, I know *of him*." Her mother paused for effect before continuing. "Your father would not consider such a liaison for his daughter and would never forgive me if I allowed that to happen. It would ruin your life," her mother said, drawing herself up.

"You had not mentioned the name, Lady Romney. As a businesswoman, I make it a practice not to indulge in gossip about those that frequent my establishment. However, it would not be wrong for me to say that Lord Butler would not be a suitable match, in my opinion, for a lovely innocent such as yourself," Mrs. Dove-Lyon finished, pinning Charlotte with her gaze.

"We have lost this season, daughter. As you are aware, you are not permitted to go to balls, lunches, or anything that spells society gatherings. It would be unseemly," her mother added.

"I see." Charlotte eyed her mother. It was a very stupid move on her part to leave Jane behind, but she did not want Uncle to hear about the near mishap and was not sure they had absolute discretion with the young girl. Charlotte wished she knew exactly how it had reached Mrs. Dove-Lyon. She could not imagine the earl's staff had already gossiped about her. Still, these were valid points. "I will hear you both out," she said finally.

"Wonderful. Here are your choices as I see them. One, you can stay with a relative of your father's—your father's sister, Lady Agatha Wendt, in Kent. You could agree to be a companion to her," Mrs. Dove-Lyon said matter-of-factly, eyeing her as she digested that distasteful option.

Aunt Agatha would be a horrible person to live with; Charlotte fought the impulse to count off the reasons why. She did not bathe regularly and used the most horrific scent to mask her own. Second, she could not hear and screamed at one for everything. Charlotte saw Mrs. Dove-Lyon raise a brow and decided she needed to stay focused and not miss any of this as it could decide her future. She wondered how much Mama had already decided on her behalf.

"A second option is to become the wife of a member of our club— a very well-placed member who is in need of a wife at the moment. He has a small boy and has suffered much since the loss of his wife a year ago."

Could she be speaking of Lord Clarendon? It certainly fit. No! It could not possibly be so. "May I ask who?" Charlotte ventured, her voice trembling.

"I am afraid not. Not at this time. I plan to discuss the opportunity with the gentleman in question. I only need your assurance that you will go through with this. We will need to get a special license and get this done without your uncle being the wiser."

Charlotte's mother sat with her mouth agape and her eyes wide. Realizing her mouth was open, she closed it before responding. "You have already determined this fine opportunity? I do not know how to thank you," she rejoined quietly.

"Lady Romney, I feel this is an excellent chance for Lady Charlotte. And there will be no financial obligation on your part for my help. I am doing it because your husband once helped guide me in my finances when my dear Colonel Lyons departed this earth. He left me in a bit of a muddle. Your husband was the only man I felt I could turn to for help. Without hesitating, he gave me direction, paving the way for his man of business to direct my affairs free of charge. I was able to save this home and other investments until my own business became profitable. I never forget a kindness."

"I do not know what to say. I know that my dear husband would not expect you to feel indebted for his kindness, but I thank you for your help. If there is ever anything I can do in return, please never hesitate to ask," her mother replied.

"Be careful, my dear. In my business, I consider all options." Mrs. Dove-Lyon chuckled.

"I am being serious. My children are my world. I am not sure what my brother is up to, but it is not benefiting my family. I need to protect them, even if they do not feel the need to be protected," her mother said. "Please know you have a friend in me."

"I will do that." The proprietress smiled. She turned to Charlotte. "Lady Charlotte, I realize that this is quite a bit to tell you, but I assure you that I have your best interests in mind. Afterall, I do have a reputation to maintain."

"You feel this is my only option?" Charlotte turned her attention to her mother.

"I do," her mother responded, wiping a tear from her eye. "One day when you have your own children, you will better understand my motivations."

"It sounds like we are agreed," Mrs. Dove-Lyon looked from mother to daughter. "Now, I suggest you both return home and get her clothes packed. Do not allow anyone in the household to assist, just in case. I would not want this to get out, and I would advise you not to be over certain of loyalties within your home. Money is a strange accomplice. It makes people do things they would not normally choose to do."

She looked at Charlotte and smiled cheekily. "From what I know of you, you will make a fine wife, and this will help your mother in other ways. Your husband—providing this match takes place, and I feel it will—will be able to petition for guardianship of your brother. That will take your uncle out of your brother's money and the estate business he is handling," she added, peering under some documents on her desk and extracting a piece of paper and a pencil. She wrote a few things on the paper and looked up. "There, now. I will make all of the arrangements. My hope is your marriage will take place in two days, no more than three. I will be in touch." She stood, signaling the meeting was at an end.

Charlotte felt dazed. Two days from now would see her married, and she had not the foggiest idea of *the identity* of her intended. She would be a Christmastide bride—a most special time to wed. However, this was not how she had ever imagined going to the altar.

CHAPTER FIVE

The next day.

Evan's insides roiled. If he had been a deeply religious man, he might have run from his house and found his way to the nearest church to repent for the activities that had brought him to this place in his life. Could things get any worse? Yesterday, he had found out that his carriage driver had almost killed a child while he was in the vehicle—and a peer, at that. To make matters worse, for the first time in a year, he found himself attracted to someone—the sister of the child his carriage nearly killed, and the sister of a friend.

Now the Widow had requested to see him. They said trouble traveled in threes. He was not sure who *they* were, but they were right. He was in trouble—triple trouble. He needed to find a fast and ready solution.

A double rap sounded on his bedroom door. It was Charles's custom to knock before he entered, and that was only a cursory one before he pushed open the door. The older man walked in with a small stack of newly pressed breeches over his right arm and a shiny pair of Hessian boots tucked under his left. "My lord, your boots are ready.

Which breeches will you wear?"

"The buff ones will suit. I suppose haste is important as I have a quick meeting on Commonwealth."

"Ah yes. The Widow." Charles drew out the last word with obvious distaste.

"How do you . . . how did—? Never mind. What do you know about it?" Evan tried to quell his own nervousness about the meeting.

"I believe you spoke of it to Lord Banbury as he was leaving." He sniffed loudly. "I have only heard she is normally expeditious in her dealings and that lives change because of her . . . er . . . *interventions*." His valet drew in a deep breath. "I hope you are not in her crosshairs, my lord."

"Since you are such an authority, what should I wear?" he asked, suddenly questioning his choice of breeches. Being called to meet with this woman had undermined his confidence without her uttering a word in his direction.

"My lord, she is but a woman. I credit you will hold your own with her. And I believe the buff breeches and the navy and gold waistcoat would add just the polish needed." His man laid the breeches on the end of the bed and extracted the waistcoat from the wardrobe. "I think this shirt will do nicely," he finished, pulling out a plain cotton shirt and frilly cravat.

Ten minutes later, Evan left his room and headed to his study. A quick drink might add just the right amount of courage. Not giving in to the voice in his head telling him to move past the liquor cabinet, he took out a clean glass and poured two fingers of his best brandy, enjoying the warm heat that traveled to his stomach. "I needed this," he muttered to himself, turning up the glass. He grabbed for another, but thought better of it, knowing there would be no allowance for tardiness.

Stanton, his footman, stepped into the room. "My lord, your carriage is waiting."

"Thank you." Why was he more nervous about this meeting than betting his pocketbook at one of her tables? A voice in his head seemed to say *because life may change*, but he rejected the answer out of hand and turned his glass up, swallowing the rest of the brandy. Mollified that there were no excuses for not showing, he followed his footman to the door and picked up his heavy coat, cane, and top hat. He would need them for the chill sure to follow.

His carriage slowed and stopped before the faded blue building that had become almost his second home over this past year. Even with its seemingly nonapparent upkeep, the building stood out among the red brick buildings that flanked it on each side. "I may as well get this over with," he muttered to himself as he stepped from the carriage. Glancing behind the footman, he noticed his new driver still in his seat. "Please inform the driver to pick me up in thirty minutes. If I am not ready, have him wait."

"Yes, my lord," the young dark-haired man replied as he closed the door behind Evan and climbed aboard the carriage.

He fired his regular driver the day before, after the man gave an appalling excuse for his almost hitting a child and not even stopping. The man told him he thought his lordship would not want to become involved and offered not even a modicum of remorse. The reserve driver had done a suitable job today. He would have Bernard promote him to lead driver and hire another reserve. *Not involved? Blast!* The damn driver made his own muddles that much worse.

A tall man Evan recognized as Titan stood scowling at the doorway and gave a quick nod to the door behind him, apparently waiting for him to enter. Burnished skin gave a rough-hewn appearance behind his unshaven face which, with the man's very thick neck and stretched clothing, added to his formidable appearance.

Suddenly I feel like a lad in short pants, he mused, passing his hat and greatcoat to another man who reached for them as the door closed. Evan followed Titan into the building, down the hall covered with a red-printed carpet to a stairway leading to the familiar smoking room and gaming rooms that overlooked the gambling floor. His destination, however, was the large ornate room in the middle, the one that always had the door closed—Mrs. Dove-Lyon's office.

"Wait here," Titan grunted. "I will let her know you have arrived." His voice hinted at displeasure before he disappeared into a smaller hall that ran off to the right.

"Certainly," Evan replied coolly, suddenly recalling Banbury informing him that Titan had seen the incident with Lady Charlotte and her brother.

Titan returned and opened the door. "Mrs. Dove-Lyon will be here soon."

If they created this reception to add to his discomfort, it scored on that point. Evan looked around the gaudy office, taking in the oversized chandelier hanging in the center of the ceiling of a room full of red velvet. He chose an overstuffed velvet chair with ornately carved arms sitting to the left of her small parlor couch. He preferred to address opponents from the left side of the room, something he recalled his father mentioning to him years before. He did not have any basis to believe it made a difference, but it had become a habit.

The opening of the door behind him and swish of petticoats alerted him that the woman had arrived, and he stood to greet her, a taut smile plastered on his face.

"Ah, Lord Clarendon. It is good to see you again. I trust you and your family are well?" she asked with a curious intonation to her voice.

It immediately reminded him of his disadvantage with this woman. He prided himself on being able to read people, but she purposely kept her face hidden. He would have to rely on the other aspects of body language and her voice to gain him any advantage in this conversation. His stomach tightened, and he drew up straighter in the chair. "My family is well, Mrs. Dove-Lyon." He paused. "I have to admit to more than a slight amount of curiosity as to the purpose of our meeting today. I am not aware of any outstanding debts," he ventured.

"As to that, all in due time," she answered, reaching to the table beside her couch and pulling out a tin of cheroots and offering him one.

"No, thank you, but I appreciate the offer. It is too early for me." Evan inclined his head politely, and she returned the metal box to the table.

"I see that you are not a man who appreciates small talk, so I will get right to the point. What I have to say will be a benefit to us both, Lord Clarendon," she continued. "Your biggest debt, if you will, is to your son. You made a rather casual wager before leaving the gaming room two days hence, which relates to that."

"Pardon? That would be curious, as I do not recall placing such a bet. I picked up my winnings and left soon after that," he supplied, outrage forming at her bringing his son into the conversation.

"Do you recall wandering to the betting book before you left?" she asked.

"No." An icy feeling shot through him. He noted the firmness to his answer, yet a sliver of memory stabbed at him, something to do with Lord Christie. The man had bought him a drink . . . no, two drinks. What happened after that?

"Are you sure?" she prompted, undeterred by his previous answer, and picked up a large brown ledger book sitting next to her.

His head ached from the combination of stress and the feeling in his bones he was about to lose serious ground.

She pulled a cord, and a youthful woman appeared. "Gertie, would you fetch us some tea and whatever the cook has in the way of sandwiches?"

"Yes, madam," the young woman replied. She curtsied and left, pulling the door closed behind her.

Evan wished he could see her face but felt sure he would not see weakness or indecision in it. However, he was having an arduous time maintaining his emotions.

"Lord Clarendon, do you recognize this?" She tugged on a thin red ribbon hanging from the bottom of the book and opened it to a page. Following the writing with her right forefinger, she drew it slowly down the page until it came to rest about two inches from the bottom. Turning the book around so he could read it, she handed it to him.

Gertie returned with tea and sandwiches and poured each of them a cup, placing them on the small tables next to them.

Squinting, he recognized his signature written in a flurry under a hand-printed statement. He stood and walked to the window that looked over the gaming room behind her parlor chair. The light from the room helped him to make out the handwriting.

The Earl of Clarendon bets that should he lose all his winnings by the end of this night, he agrees to allow the House to choose his wife.

Signed: The Earl of Clarendon
Witnessed: Titus

"That is a stupid bet. It *has* to be a joke," he exclaimed. "You cannot hold me to that. I would have had to be deep in my cups to sign such a thing," he responded, unease seeping into his stomach. He needed to leave the room, convinced that another shoe was about to drop. Feeling invincible at cards that night and having won against tremendous odds, he had bragged to Lord Christie about always winning, except in life. Lord Christie had been equally in his cups, he felt sure—too much to have concocted such a bet.

He looked up at the Widow and caught a wide smile of red lips beneath her black veil.

"I assure you it is no joke." She studied him. "I see you are re-calling this," she spoke as she pulled the book back and closed it, its ribbon still in place. "Titan overheard you make the statement and asked you if you wanted to make that a wager. You accepted and lost," she said with decisiveness. "That is your signature, is it not?"

Damn it. As soon as she mentioned Titan, he remembered signing the book, and that was problematic. He was trapped by his own arrogance. "Where exactly is this going?" he asked, an edge to his voice.

"Relax, Lord Clarendon. I do not believe its direction will displease you." She fiddled with her sleeves, adjusting the lace to cover her hands. "I hear that you will *finally* assume the care of your son from your sister's home. A wife would be perfect, and I have just the person in mind."

"Where do you get off—" he stopped and began again, his tone less heated. "Surely, you do not expect me to abide by—"

"I do." She cut him off. "You compromised this young lady after almost running over her brother with your carriage on your way here. My man witnessed the episode. Had you not already been soused, you would have demanded your driver stop, but you drove on, leaving both the little boy and his sister injured."

"How do you know of this?" he demanded.

"I have ears. Let us leave it at that. The young lady spent a lengthy period in your house without a chaperone just two days ago, and her mother is most aggrieved that she will be quite ruined in the eyes of the *ton*. Lady Charlotte Grisham will make a beautiful wife, and I believe over time, you may come to appreciate her attributes."

He started to speak but stopped himself, realizing the prospect of the spirited woman becoming his wife excited him. "And if I agree to this, it will be a marriage of convenience. That is what she wants?" He could not believe it. The woman had beauty and wealth—at least he thought she did—was witty and did not speak of the weather as all other debutantes did.

"The young woman's father did me a kindness many years ago, and I seek to do his family a good turn." She let out a long easy breath.

"You are willing?"

Evan remained silent for a few minutes with his gaze locked on the veiled woman across from him. "This appears to have been a setup." She started to speak, but he held up his right hand in acquiescence and chuckled lightly.

"You find this is amusing, my lord?" she inquired in a serious tone, tilting her head slightly.

"No, I do not. Not really," he began. "What I find amusing is something my valet occasionally tells me. 'Be careful what you wish for,' he says. This is one of those times I suppose I should have not wished for anything."

"You wished for a wife?" she replied, incredulous.

"No. I assure you, that never entered my mind. I did, however, wish for a solution." A rueful smile tugged at his lips.

"Ah." She smiled, although it looked more like a sneer, and gave an abrupt incline of her head. "Then we have an understanding. The wedding will take place as soon as you procure a special license. Send word that you have it. It will be a private ceremony the day after tomorrow, at ten in the morning at St. George's Chapel. I have already made arrangements."

He sat stunned for a long minute. "You were sure I would agree to this," he stated flatly, not expecting an answer. Yet rather than feeling his life continuing to spin out of control, he felt hopeful. *Oddly* hopeful.

The woman stood to leave but stopped and turned to him. "One more thing, my lord," she said with firmness in her voice. "It is my advice that you do not discuss this wedding with anyone outside of those you trust with your life. I believe the lady's uncle does not wish the best for her," she said caustically, pausing. "Should this wedding become foiled by the uncle, please be advised that according to the wager you signed, the House may choose a wife. I may not be as generous with my next selection. This is a business."

CHAPTER SIX

LADY CHARLOTTE LAY in her bed with her covers pulled to her chin and stared up at her ceiling, thinking. She felt chilled, but not because of the cold rain outside her window. Rather, she was unable to reconcile how her life had changed so in the past two days. By this time tomorrow, not only would she be a wife to a man she had only just met, she would be a mother as well. Worse, there was nothing she could do but accept her fate.

Her mother had received a missive from Mrs. Dove-Lyon that all had been accepted and arranged. Charlotte would be Lady Clarendon, the wife of an earl, with all of the responsibilities she had seen Mama perform for Papa.

The visit with her mother to the Lyon's Den had been eye opening. She had no idea there was a matchmaker in London, and not once had she considered her family was acquainted with such a woman. Further, Charlotte had never considered *she* would need such a service. Unsure of how Mrs. Dove-Lyon had accomplished it, all plans discussed on her visit with her mother were in motion.

For her part, Charlotte had made the poor decision to take matters into her own hands and confront the earl; consequently, she had only herself to blame for the predicament she found herself in. Mama had been the biggest surprise. For months, she had worried about her mother's state of mind over the loss of Papa, only to realize her mother had been playacting to fool her uncle, whom no one trusted.

Charlotte glanced over at the pale lavender chiffon dress draped over the chair in front of her fireplace. The sleeves were trimmed in double rolls of white satin, and the lacy bottom fanned out like a flower on the pink and white rug, embellished in ecru Belgian lace. It was a lovely dress. She had first worn it for her introduction to society, and now it would be her wedding dress. He mother had told her she looked like a princess and assured her that Papa would understand her not wearing black to her wedding. Perhaps she would feel like that wearing it again.

It must do. There was no time for a seamstress to create a new dress. Luckily, everything still fit, and the style was still as stunning as it was when she first wore it.

A quick rap sounded at her door.

"Come in," she said, wishing whomever it was would leave her alone and let her spend her day moping. It might be the last such day for a while to come. She sighed. "I may as well get up. I know better than to think I could just be lazy." She pulled the covers back and swung her feet over the side of the bed, searching for her slippers.

"Lady Charlotte, this package came for you." Jane, her lady's maid, nodded to a small package sitting on the left side of a silver tray, while her hot chocolate and toast sat on the right.

"Who sent it to me? Did they leave a card?"

"No card arrived with it. A courier delivered it. 'Tis exciting!" she gushed, handing the package to Charlotte.

Charlotte turned the package over, examining it. A plain brown wrapper secured by twine gave no hints as to whom had sent it. A red wax seal of a flower added nothing remarkable, as she knew no one or nothing associated with the symbol. Deciding to open it when she was alone, she reached for the cup of chocolate. "I am famished. Perhaps it would be more prudent to drink my chocolate, first. I have been dreaming of a hot cup of chocolate, and I do not want it to get cold." Raising the cup to her lips, she tasted. "Mmm. Perfect." It *was* just what she needed. "Would you be a dear, Jane, and draw me a bath?" Charlotte asked before she took a second sip of the hot drink.

"Yes, my lady. Right away." The petite maid curtsied and went to organize the bath.

She had about thirty minutes while they were heating the water. Charlotte set down her cup of chocolate and grabbed the small package. Untying the twine and unwrapping it, she pulled out a small green velvet case with a folded note.

Dearest Charlotte,

Please accept this small token of my esteem. I realize this is not the wedding you desire, but I believe in the vows dictated by marriage and will be a faithful husband. I find myself looking forward to our union.

Please wear this tomorrow for our ceremony. I saw this and immediately thought of you.

Truly,

E

"How thoughtful and totally unexpected," she whispered to herself as she gingerly opened the green velvet box. A gold emerald and diamond ring and matching bracelet glittered up at her. The ring had a large oval emerald nestled in a circle of small diamonds set in a delicate gold band. *He picked this out for me.* Charlotte felt a fluttering in the pit of her stomach. She had never seen a more beautiful combination of stones. She started to place the ring on her finger when she heard Jane's voice in the hall. Her bath!

Quickly, she scooped up the paper, box, twine, and jewelry and shoved them in the back of the drawer to her nightstand. Seeing the note had fluttered to the floor, she snatched it up and put it inside, pushing a small book in front of it all and shutting the drawer just as Jane and several servants behind her came into the room with her tub and water. Stepping in front of the small table, she touched the drawer, making sure it was closed, her hands hidden by the folds of her dress.

"Your bath is ready, my lady," the diminutive maid said, placing a small cake of jasmine-scented soap and a towel on the table and wiping her hands on her white apron.

"Thank you, Jane. I would like a few minutes by myself to soak and get rid of the chill I feel. Perhaps you should come back in about twenty minutes to help me with my dress. Thank you for the soap. I love the smell of jasmine in the winter."

"Yes, my lady. Allow me a few moments to tend to your fire." Jane grabbed the poker and stoked the glowing embers in the fireplace into a more robust flame, instantly warming that side of the room. "Shall I hang this dress, my lady?" Jane pointed to the dress she had chosen for the wedding, still laying across the chair.

Dash it all! I forgot to put the dress away. Charlotte recalled Mrs. Dove-Lyon's warning. With all the nonchalance she could muster, Charlotte responded. "Yes. I saw it hanging in the wardrobe and could not resist trying it on to see if it still fit, just to recall that wonderful day. However, the mood has passed. Please hang it for me." She kept her voice steady.

"Certainly, my lady. It will be nice when you are able to wear more than mourning attire." Jane picked up the dress, shook out the wrinkles, and hung it in the wardrobe. "If you decide to wear it again, I will press it for you. The lace is so beautiful," she fawned, fingering the edges as she tucked the garment into the closet. "I understand the need for privacy, my lady. I will give you time for your bath. Let me know if you need anything else," she added, leaving and pulling the door closed behind her.

Charlotte had only a little time, but she waited until they left, then pulled out the note to read it once more. "I had not expected this," she murmured, running her fingers over the dried ink. It seemed he planned to give their union a chance. A smile tugged the corner of her mouth. Hastily, she reached for the ring and placed it on her finger. She had never imagined receiving a wedding gift from him, much less anything so thoughtful. His beautiful gesture warmed her heart. Sliding the ring onto her fourth finger, she held up her hand, turning it various angles and admiring it. *I wish I had time to try both pieces on, but with Jane hovering, I need to hurry through my bath.*

Wistfully, she folded the note and placed it in the box with the jewelry, carefully sliding them all into the back of her drawer and adding two small tomes in front of it to keep the gift hidden. Then she readied herself for her bath and slipped into the warm water, relaxing against the back of the tub. The jasmine soap smelled delightful. She lathered up her hands, washing first her legs, then her arms before moving to the rest of her body.

Closing her eyes, Charlotte sunk further into the water and contemplated her future once more. Something could be said for being the wife of a wealthy earl. Perhaps Mama and Jason could come and live with her, at least until she was certain that her new husband could gain guardianship over her brother. Nibbling her lower lip, she realized with renewed clarity the value of the gift her Evan had just sent her. It was a promise of protection, something she needed at this time in her life. They needed each other for different reasons, she mused.

When did he become Evan to her? She recalled having heard his first marriage was a love match. She thought about the gift and the note. *This will be a marriage of convenience, but could there be a chance for more?* What about his drinking? The image of her brother almost getting hit by his carriage flashed through her mind. She needed to forgive him to allow their marriage a proper chance. Could she?

Lingering, she waited until the water was almost cold before finally standing and drying herself. She needed to protect the opportunity Mrs. Dove-Lyon had secured for her and was determined to look at her impending nuptials differently.

Jane would be back in mere minutes. Charlotte credited this as the most enjoyable bath she could remember. She craved the solitude, wishing she had a little more time to reread the note Evan had written her. Distractedly, she tried out his name on her lips. "Evan." She enjoyed the sound and the way it rolled off her tongue so easily. She could admit to an attraction to him, although she was unwilling to concede it to anyone else, especially him. *Is it contrived?* she wondered. Could there possibly be a chance for the two of them in a marriage forced by convenience? Should she speak with him about the alcohol?

Loud voices coming from downstairs heralded her uncle's arrival. She heard a strange voice. Did he have someone with him? Worried but not understanding why, she rushed herself from the tub and drew behind the screen in her room. Next time she bathed, she would have Jane place this between the tub and the door. *There will be no next time, ninny. You will be married*, she chastised herself. Adjusting to her new circumstances was proving difficult.

Footsteps stomped up to the door. *Her uncle!* She threw her chemise over her head, shivering from not being able to fully dry. At least the room had warmed.

Three raps on the door announced Jane, who slipped into the room and turned the lock on the door behind her. "It is me, my lady," she whispered loudly. "Your uncle is here and is demanding to see you in the study. I locked the door behind me in case he forgot himself."

"Thank you, Jane. I cannot imagine what he wants with me. *Umph!* Can you help me with this?" Charlotte stopped trying to pull the laces to her corset and turned around for Jane.

Jane began securing the corset strings.

Charlotte leaned against the doorframe and could feel the familiar routine of the laces being tightened one space at a time. Jane was fast.

"Lean in, and I will slide the dress over your head." Jane had selected a muted gray merino trimmed in lace with three delicate rows of small seed pearls centered on the bodice. The sleeves were loose and gathered at the wrist with a small band of lace on the bottom. The dress fell perfectly over her curves.

Once the back ribbon was secured, Charlotte began to feel warmer. "Can we put my hair up in a simple fashion? I think I should have washed it, but with the commotion downstairs, I rushed out of the tub to begin dressing."

"Yes, my lady, I will pull it up into a chignon with some curls."

The doorknob jiggled, followed by a loud knock. "Lady Charlotte, are you in there?"

It was her uncle. "I am not presentable at the moment, Uncle."

A loud harrumph. "See that you show yourself in five minutes in my study."

Papa's study, she contradicted silently, furrowing her brow in anger. "Yes, Uncle." She kept her tone flat. *What could this be about?*

"There you go, my lady." Jane stepped back, pleased with her work. She grabbed the silver-backed looking glass and held it up from behind Charlotte's head so she could see her hair in her mirror.

"I have never seen this particular style, Jane. You are always so efficient and make my hair look lovely! You are such a treasure," Charlotte murmured as she studied her perfection.

"You best slip your shoes on and get downstairs, my lady. I will tidy your room."

Charlotte gave a quick glance to her nightstand, satisfied that she had hidden her gift. Jane had forgotten to ask about it, something which now pleased her to no end. She was not in the habit of lying to her family and staff and felt a bit in over her head today. Pinching her cheeks, she stepped into a pair of gray satin slippers. Giving a quick tremulous smile at Jane, she rushed out the door and down the stairs.

"Charlotte!" Mama whispered her name loudly from a slight crack in the parlor door.

She stopped and stood near the door. "Do you know what Uncle is wanting?" Charlotte whispered. Her body felt taut with tension.

"I believe I overheard him say something about you being out without a chaperone. I would come with you, but if I do, he will know my wits are about me. Disagree with him and tell him he is mistaken. I am sorry to tell you to lie, but he is up to mischief. It will take him time to track down the truth, and we will be on our way by morning. Trust me," her mother whispered before pushing back from the door and closing it.

Nervous, Charlotte took a deep breath and relaxed her shoulders. Matt had taught her that. She wished with all her heart that he was there. None of this would be happening if he was. Her brother had always been her hero. She could use a hero right now. Evan's face flashed in her mind, and she squeezed her eyes shut as if that would erase it. Summoning her courage, she squared her shoulders and opened the door to her father's study.

"Ah, there you are," her uncle bellowed. It was unusual for him to yell. He sounded oddly nervous, as if something had gone wrong. "Sit," he demanded, walking to the brandy decanter and pouring himself a measure. Turning with the glass, he walked to the front of the desk and leaned against it in front of the chair she occupied.

"Yes?" She focused on his chin, deciding that she could keep a cooler demeanor if her entire being could focus. It worked as a child to focus on Papa's eyes. But Uncle was not nearly as nice, and she preferred the chin, hoping he didn't dribble his brandy because she would laugh.

"It has come to my attention that two days ago, you were seen in a carriage belonging to Lord Clarendon." He narrowed his gaze at her as he drew a sip from the glass.

Charlotte narrowed her own eyes, quickly deciding that taking the offensive was the better position and summoning up enough ire and indignation to address the man. She took a chance on their staff that no one here would have reported her to him. Therefore, it had to be someone outside the house. She would focus on who later. The shade had mostly been down, except for when they had driven through Mayfair.

For now, she would call his bluff. "No, Uncle. How . . . *why* would I do that? And *who* would say such a thing?" she demanded, mindful not to overplay her position. She needed to give him enough pause to question his source. This was not a conversation in which she wanted to participate. She hated deception, but she was learning that surviving as a woman within the confines of *ton* mores was an education in itself. Careful not to lose her contact with his chin, she kept her eyes steady.

He quirked a dark eyebrow at her. "I see . . ." he responded, still staring at her. He looked down into his glass and took another swig before walking back to his desk chair and sitting.

Charlotte sensed she had won that small battle. He looked skeptical and puzzled, probably at both her and his source. "Who would say that? I have done no such thing!"

"Relax, gel. For now, let us put it aside," the baron huffed. "I have something to tell you. If your mother was not mourning so much, I would say she should be here, but as it is, she is not right. That is a problem for another day. I have a visitor that will be here at ten tomorrow. And I want you looking your best."

"May I ask who your guest will be since it affects me?" she asked flatly.

"You may. Lord Burton will be here tomorrow. He has inquired of you, and I believe him to hold some interest."

Charlotte controlled her repulsion. Lord Burton may be a marquess, but he was reputed to be a cruel toady. This confirmed he was the person Mama had overheard her uncle speaking with regarding a betrothal. Fighting back the bile that surfaced in her throat, she summoned a reply. "I am not acquainted with Lord Burton. How did he come to know of me?" she asked in a soft voice.

He harrumphed and eyed her critically. "I am not sure where he met you. Certainly a question for me to ask before the papers are signed," he added, giving a sardonic laugh. "But he is most anxious to meet you."

"Is that all?" She wanted to flee as far as her feet would carry her.

"Yes, gel. But I am curious about one thing," he said as she stood to leave. "You did not say you had *not* met Lord Clarendon in your denial." His voice was laced with suspicion.

"You did not ask if I knew of Lord Clarendon. You accused me of riding in his carriage," she responded coolly.

"You always were a cagey one." He sneered. "Do you . . . *know* him?"

"I know who Lord Clarendon is by reputation. His wife died fairly recently, is that correct?"

"Yes. Quite right. His wife died giving birth to their son. However, my opinion is he is not an honorable man and should be avoided. You get my inference, I feel sure. You are a smart one—too smart for your own good, if you ask me," he added, glowering at her. "I believe we understand each other."

Charlotte shuddered at the cruelty her uncle exposed. "Yes, Uncle. Quite sure that we do. Is that all?" She felt the uncontrollable urge to flee his presence. She had barely skated by his inquisition and needed air.

"It is. Close the door behind you," he replied gruffly, dismissing her with a wave of his hand as he swigged the last of the brandy in his glass.

Charlotte summoned all the will she possessed to remain calm and maintain her decorum, determined to walk slowly to the parlor. Looking around, she whispered to her mother. "Mama, please wait here, and I will come to you when he leaves." Tears pricked the corners of her eyes. Picking up her skirts, she moved upstairs as quickly as possible and closed the door to her room.

CHAPTER SEVEN

U PON LEAVING THE Lyon's Den, Evan had ridden first to Banbury's townhouse and told him of the upcoming nuptials, then together they went straight to Dean's office. His man of business assured them he could pull information together and deliver all he could find by early the next afternoon.

Not known for his trusting nature, Evan stared at the envelope with Dean's report concerning Baron Langdale. The whole marriage business had stirred his curiosity to take a closer look at everyone involved in this union. Banbury sat across from him in his study as he held the packet and reflected. "Yesterday was the first night in a long time that I failed to attend the Den to drink or play games."

"I am sure your body and your wallet thank you." Banbury snorted, then inclined his head toward the packet. "What does it say, Clarendon?" His friend swirled his scotch, then took a long sip.

Evan took his letter opener and ran it along the edge of the packet, then pulled out the documents. "Hmm. This is rather enlightening. I had expected a delay in receiving this, but Dean's association with Lord Romney's affairs helped immensely. He had much information at his fingertips."

"What does it say?" Banbury interjected, sitting up a little straighter.

He read further. "We were right. The baron is spending as much of Romney's money as he can. It appears checks have been written to his own estate and others to people well-known in the investment arena. These monies could be covering debts he created dabbling with stocks." He absently rolled the handle of his wax stamp in his hand while he read. "No, it is worse than I thought. Dean traced Langdale's losses, and it appears the man lost quite a lot of money in the slave trade. I cannot feel sorry for him. Langdale bought part interest in a shipping company known to be heavily involved in slave trading."

"I say, that sounds unfortunate," his friend said.

"Indeed. Since the wars have concluded, much of Europe have added their muscle to the enforcement of the Slave Trade Act, and hopefully together, they will put an end to the whole nasty business. Shipping companies such as his are suffering badly." Evan passed the report to Banbury and leaned back against his desk, folding his arms.

Banbury perused the statement for a few moments. "What do you make of this notation on the bottom of Dean's report?" He edged closer to his friend, pointing to a post about a visit from Lord Thomas Burton. "That does not seem good to me. The marquess is known for his cruelty and womanizing. I try to never share the same air space with the man."

"Is he married?" Evan heard himself ask. *Something feels wrong here.*

"No. There was a widow years ago that he was rumored to be involved with. Some speculated they would marry, but I believe she died suddenly. Tragic, really. There was some scandal about her death, but no one was charged. Let me think." Banbury sat back in the leather chair and stared at the ceiling before rocking forward and landing his chair on all legs. "Lady Paula James, the widow of Viscount James, who died several years ago," he said in an excited voice. "I knew if I thought about it a moment, I could recall it."

"I recollect that, although the details of her death evade me," Evan murmured. "So, will you stand up for me?" he asked, redirecting the conversation and smiling at his friend. "You have not answered me, and I asked yesterday." He laughed good naturedly.

"I would be honored." Banbury watched him. "You are looking forward to this. I can see it, and I am stunned. Three days ago, I would have sworn you would never marry again. Ha! I think I will stay away from the Lyon's Den. I am not ready to get caught by the parson's noose." He guffawed.

"I cannot say I am thrilled about it, no." Evan took a small sip of the scotch he had been nursing all morning. "But after the week I have had, I can see reason that it could benefit my life at this time. The woman is not Amelia, but she is interesting. And given time, I think we could rub along well." He spoke thoughtfully, looking at his friend.

"There is nothing that says you cannot find happiness a second time, with another woman. Losing Amelia was dreadful, but this woman is no wilting daisy. You need a woman who can challenge you. My opinion." Banbury grinned.

"True. However, I am not looking for a great love story here. Just someone to take care of Edward. He arrives the day after tomorrow, and I need to structure a better household to care for the lad."

In truth, he did not want a marriage of convenience, having known love. But there was little choice. He was not sure if he was ready for a wife, but he needed to find a solution. Mrs. Dove-Lyon had handed him one. A marriage of convenience could be a worthwhile start. He realized he wanted to try to make it more, if possible, and it motivated him to select and send a gift to Charlotte. It was the first time he had thought of her as Charlotte.

"I sent her a wedding gift this morning and am curious as to whether she received it. I had a special messenger deliver it. I disguised the seal with one I think my sister used occasionally."

"I would never have expected that of you," his friend said. "I think that was the right thing to have done."

"Look!" Evan pointed to a paragraph on the next page. "Dean notes that her uncle inquired about her dowry. That makes me suspicious, considering all of *this*," he said, rattling the papers and slapping them down on the corner of his desk. "What do you say to an early dinner? I can have Cook pull together a decent meal, and perhaps we can talk about the arrangements for tomorrow. I do not plan to go to the Lyon's Den this evening."

Banbury grew sober. "You know this is Matthew's sister— Matthew, our friend," he emphasized. "We may not have Matthew to answer to, but I want your word that you will treat her with respect," Banbury asked, a note of contempt in his voice.

"Relax, Christopher. I have no intentions of dishonoring my new wife, regardless of whether our relationship improves beyond the merits of suitability."

The door opened, and both men quit the conversation.

"My lord, you have a missive." Bernard entered and held out a silver salver with the sealed note on it. "It was delivered a few minutes ago by a young man who said he worked for the Romney household."

Evan lifted the note and opened it. "That will be all, Bernard." The butler started to leave. "*Wait*," Evan stopped him. He read the note and looked up at his friend. "How unusual. The note is from Lady Charlotte's mother. She indicates that Langdale plans to betroth her daughter to Lord Burton tomorrow. She asks if I can arrange something to help." He glanced up at his butler. "Has her messenger left, Bernard?"

"No, my lord. He said he needs to return with a reply." Bernard stood at attention with the salver in front of him.

"Give me a moment to draft a reply. I will bring it to you," Evan said.

"Of course, my lord. I will let the young man know," he said, turning and leaving the room.

"Allow me to pick up your bride. I have a carriage without any emblem, and I will ride with my men. This seems a bit coincidental to me—not on the ladies' part, but on the part of Langdale. I do not like the man. He is a bottom feeder." Banbury spoke softly to his friend. "We do not want a hitch on your wedding day," he added.

Evan guffawed at the timing of his friend's joke. It was part of Banbury's charm that he could diffuse a tense situation. "I fear you are right. They are asking for a time that is not even respectable. Can you do this?" He smirked in his friend's direction.

"I will do it for you, Clarendon. Of course! And after I see you wed, I will take my leave and catch up on my rest." He snorted.

"Then it is settled. I will pen that you will arrive at six o'clock tomorrow morning to pick them up. If you do not mind, I will follow and conceal myself once we are on their property. It is bad luck to see your wife before the wedding, and I have had enough of that, so I will rely on you to get her safely into the carriage. But I do not want to invite bad luck by not being careful with the baron. I want to be there."

"That works," Banbury agreed. "I understand your sentiment; however, I think that is an old wives' tale about not seeing the bride. Then again, if things go badly, your bad luck will be that Mrs. Dove-Lyon still has you within her parson's snare. Her next pick might have a terrible . . ." He paused. "Disposition," he finished with a grin.

Evan penned the instructions and pulled the other wax emblem from his drawer. It was the one he had used earlier for the wedding gift. Dripping the wax, he sealed it and took it to Bernard. "Please have this delivered to Lady Charlotte Grisham," he instructed, ignoring the idea of sending it to her mother. If the mother's concern was legitimate, surely his bride would be aware of it as well.

"Right away, my lord." Bernard left the two men alone.

"You distrust everyone these days, Clarendon," Banbury quizzed when the door closed.

"Let us say I am suspicious of this whole situation, and I will endeavor to trust my wife. At least I will try," he said, pouring himself a small measure of scotch and passing the decanter to his friend. "Have you spoken to your investigative friend . . . Sinclair? I wish to try to find Matthew. If her uncle is as cagey as I think, we may have difficulty removing him from the young lord's guardianship. Finding Matthew would help that. He is their heir, after all."

"You would also supply an acceptable guardian, Clarendon," supplied Banbury. "I sent word for Sinclair to meet with me. He sent me a missive that I found very interesting."

"Please do not keep me in suspense," prompted Evan.

"Sinclair was engaged for a short period by Romney to find his son. Shortly after the earl's death, he was sent word to abort the search. I could speculate on who sent those orders, but I think in all fairness, we should meet with Sinclair and get the firsthand information," Banbury quipped.

"I could never have had this level of good timing and fortune at a gaming table," he said with astonishment. *Even though I do mostly win.* It still rankled him that he lost a wager at the Lyon's Den and did not have a clear memory of said loss. Still, he found it hard to be downcast about it, although a small part of him wondered how much money he bet double or nothing.

"I am not so surprised, considering there are only a few credible investigators being used and the elder Lord Romney would have used his connections to locate Sinclair. He is the best, by far. He will be in London in three days and asked if we could meet him at White's for lunch."

"I will be newly married, but I believe I can manage," Evan said. "As part of my renewed effort to change, I have engaged a decorator to meet with my countess. I will move the meeting up to correspond with this and doubt I will be missed."

Banbury pushed back from the table. "I must go if I am to get enough rest. We will save your bachelor's celebration for a post marriage one, if you will."

"Sure. But you gave me one the first time I married." Evan laughed. He realized that he had spoken several times of his first marriage without the pain he was used to feeling, and he had not been in his cups. *Was it possible to put that pain and sorrow behind?*

"Yes. So we did give you a party. Are you saying you have gotten too old to celebrate?" Banbury goaded.

"Of course not. I miss the fun we had with Matthew—the three of us and Lucas. The *four musketeers*, we called ourselves. It would be nice to feel that unencumbered again." He sighed. "Matthew was much more grounded than the rest of us. I hope we can find him, as much for my future wife as for myself—for us. I had not realized how much I missed the camaraderie of our small group," Evan mused.

"It is almost dinner time. I think I should go home and get things ready." Banbury stood to take his leave.

"No, stay, please. Consider it my stag night." He grinned. "I am sure that Cook has made plenty."

"You have a dinner guest, then."

The two men snickered and headed in the direction of the kitchen.

CHAPTER EIGHT

A S SOON AS Jane left her room, Charlotte slid from her bed. Shortly before dinner, Charlotte had received a short missive from Evan explaining the arrangements and giving an introduction to his friend, the Earl of Banbury, who would be helping them. Putting her blue velvet robe on over her shift, she grabbed the traveling bag from the bottom of her wardrobe and carefully packed the lavender dress among the rest of her items. Then she set the bag aside and began to dress herself.

As quickly as possible, she slid on her corset and pulled the strings tight, determined to maintain some semblance of respectability. She wished she could have left her corset overnight on for ease, but there was no way to do that with Jane assisting her. Quickly, she chose gray sateen with delicate silver-lace edging that secured with silver ribbons. She carefully dressed in her hose, shoes, and undergarment assembly, then set the ribbons so she could pull them taut by herself. When she had finished struggling into the dress, she felt ready.

Charlotte started to leave but turned back. Her gift! Quietly, she opened her bedside drawer, reaching into the back and grabbing her note and the small green jewelry box. Opening it, she carefully placed the emerald ring on the familiar gold necklace she wore around her neck, pleased to have it slide next to the small locket containing miniature pictures of her parents and two brothers.

Satisfied she had everything necessary, Charlotte opened her door and looked up and down the dark hall for any signs that someone would still be awake. Seeing none, she held her bag tight and tiptoed downstairs. The bag was small enough that she was able to hide it in Mama's parlor behind a large potted plant that stood in the corner behind a wingback chair. It would be a good spot to wait. She could keep an ear open for the carriage and quickly grab her bag from its hiding place. Making sure the door was closed tightly, she sat in the chair and closed her eyes to wait for her mother where they had agreed.

Mama had decided to bring Jason with them, not comfortable leaving him in case her uncle came earlier and discovered their duplicity. Hopefully the man would not discover where they had gone. Both of them had kept quiet on their plans, sharing them with no one except each other.

She checked the time on the hallway clock. There were only three more hours before they were to leave. Nibbling her lower lip, she wondered how she would manage this day on so little sleep.

Charlotte closed her eyes, and within minutes dozed into a light sleep. In her dreams she and the Earl of Clarendon stood at the door to a large room, holding hands and smiling at each other while they welcomed guests to a Christmastide feast. Long tapered beeswax candles in two large golden chandeliers illuminated a room decked out with seasonal greenery. Beautiful china and stemware decorated long tables draped in white tablecloths. Food of every sort was being brought into the room and placed on serving tables against a far wall with wonderful aromas wafting her way. "Mmm."

"Charlotte. Wake up." Her mother shook her shoulders. "'Tis time to leave. There is a man approaching the door. I believe our carriage is here."

Charlotte blinked and looked into the blue-green eyes of her mother, who was smiling at her, and the half-awake ones of her little brother. "Mama. Jason. Sorry, I must have dozed."

"You were having a delicious dream, daughter," her mother whispered playfully. "You were licking your lips. You must share your dream when we are away."

"Oh! I cannot recall the dream. I do feel hungry," she divulged slowly. She did remember seeing the food in her dream, a point brought home to her by the grumbling in her stomach. She had been so nervous the evening before that she barely allowed herself to eat, afraid she might become ill. That decision was coming back to haunt her with pangs of hunger. "I am sorry. I think I might be hungry," she said sheepishly. "Let us hurry if they are here."

Charlotte grabbed their pelisses and Jason's coat and hat from the cloak stand, feeling in the pockets for her kid gloves. Mama said that was the best place to keep a spare pair, just in case. If this was anything, it was *just in case*.

Jason said nothing as his mother and sister ushered them from the house, each carrying a small bag.

A tall blond-haired man met them at the bottom of the steps to her home. "I am the Earl of Banbury," he whispered his introduction to Charlotte, her mother, and her brother. "Let us be off. Clarendon waits for us just beyond the gate with the carriage. We chose not to pull it up close to the house."

She could see the black carriage with a footman standing beside an opened door, and she breathed easily, realizing they would make it away from the house without discovery. A man on horseback cantered up beside the carriage, and she recognized Lord Clarendon.

"Warming bricks and thick covers await you. We do not have far to go. We are going to Banbury's townhouse, which, like yours, has a small gated yard in front of it for privacy. We will leave from there for the ceremony at the chapel," Clarendon said, his gaze fixed on Charlotte.

Charlotte wanted to thank him for the presents—but not in front of Mama. When her mother's head turned, she carefully pulled the necklace out of her collar and showed him the ring. He smiled and gave an appreciative tilt of his head. *He has a nice smile.*

As the carriage lurched forward, both women relaxed against the dark leather squabs.

"I feel like a girl again, slipping out under the cover of night." Mama chortled.

What did her mother just say? "Mama, you and Papa slipped out? I should be shocked!" Charlotte feigned an indignant tone, and both women giggled. It felt good to be able to breathe, unfettered by the fear of discovery. "I admit to feeling a little nervous. I do not know him, Mama." Charlotte worried her lip.

"Darling daughter, I am sorry to have had to play this hand, but without Papa, I feared for your safety. I overheard your uncle and Lord Burton. He is not a nice man, and I would not have wished you married to him. I had no idea what to do, not until you came home in Lord Clarendon's carriage. It is for the best," she added, leaning over and squeezing Charlotte's hand.

Charlotte felt manipulated but was not angry with Mama. She was taking care of her the same way Charlotte had been taking care of Jason when she had visited Lord Clarendon.

The carriage slowed and turned into a bricked driveway. The two men handed their horses to a waiting stable hand and stood ready when the door to the carriage opened.

"Thank you, Lord Banbury. We are most appreciative," her mother intoned as he handed her out of the carriage.

"Mama, where are we?" Jason asked, wiping his eyes and looking at the large gray stone townhouse.

"Your sister is getting married today, my darling. We are here to celebrate," Mama answered smoothly.

"Will Uncle be coming?" he asked as he leaned toward the doorway, his voice trembling.

"No, my dear, your uncle has some appointments he must attend to," she answered her son. "Let us go inside." She helped him stand and handed him off to Lord Banbury, who was at the door.

Charlotte wondered about her brother's question asked in a voice tinged with fear. She had heard Uncle address him with a sharp tone, but she wondered if there had been more unseen.

Lord Banbury placed Jason down on the brick driveway and surveyed the small group as the carriage doors were closed behind them. "We have a few hours before we need to be at the chapel. I have made arrangements for the carriage to pick us up at nine. My housekeeper, Mrs. Plume, stands just inside the door, ladies. She will lead you to rooms to allow you to freshen up or take a quick nap, whatever is your pleasure. If anyone would like to break their fast, the food is being placed in the small dining room on the right of the main hallway. Thomas can lead the way." He gave a slight wave to indicate a tall gentleman with salt and pepper hair and silver sideburns standing at the door.

The butler bowed. "It is my pleasure to see that you have everything you need, my lord and ladies."

Charlotte's heart fluttered as he walked toward her. She found him handsome, but with all that had taken place these past days, she had given herself time to take full measure of the man. His dark brown hair was fashionably cut above his ears and complimented his stylish attire. He wore his black greatcoat opened at the front to reveal a burgundy waistcoat over a burgundy shirt and black cravat hugging a lean upper body, while his black breeches and Hessian boots emphasized his muscular legs. He held his gloved hand out, and she placed hers in his palm.

"I apologize, my lady, for the secrecy," Evan said sincerely, locking his gaze with Charlotte's. "However, I am familiar with your uncle and his tactics. He will most likely discover you gone in an hour or so. We will be using Banbury's carriage to the church. My carriage will be waiting at the chapel by the time we leave, allowing us to ride to my home. Langdale will have no recourse at that point because you will be a married woman."

His voice was soft and laced with concern. He was all tenderness, which helped soothe her frayed nerves.

"Come, let us go inside out of this cold damp weather." He guided her into the front parlor. "We will leave the door open, but there are a few things I feel a need to say to you."

A footman followed behind with their bags.

Charlotte felt herself begin to thaw. "My lord, I appreciate all that you have done. And I apologize for my bullheadedness in charging to your townhouse the other day. Had I known this would result, I might have handled things differently." Her voice sounded quiet and tense, even to her ears. She caught the insult she had just delivered and struggled to correct her faux pas. "My lord, that was not the way I meant it. I did not mean that there was something wrong with marrying you. I meant marrying you in this . . . rush."

He gave her a smile that melted her heart and took her hand in his. "Nonsense, my dear. While we find ourselves forced into a marriage of convenience, it is not one of your making." He laughed sardonically. "I must admit to misdeeds of my own while under the heady influence of drink, a habit of late that I am taking pains to correct. It appears that I made a silly wager and played into the Widow's hand. It dabbles in making matches. I was well aware of that, but thought myself immune to her tricks. It seems I was not."

What is he trying to say? Charlotte sensed profound regret on his part, forcing a knot to form in her throat as a wave of heat worked its way up her neck.

"However," he continued, "I will admit to looking forward to our nuptials."

"You are?" she asked in a low shaky voice.

"I am," he soothed. "I am no poet but attempted to tell you this with a note and my gift. Was it to your liking?"

"Oh yes, my lord. It is beautiful." She moved her sleeve up and displayed the bracelet hanging from her wrist. "I have never owned anything so elegant."

"I am pleased," he said, touching her neck slowly and pulling the chain into view. "May I?"

Unsure of what he meant, she merely nodded.

He opened the clasp, removed the ring, and secured the necklace around her neck again. Taking the ring, he removed the light gray kid glove from her left hand and placed the ring on her fourth finger. "There. The fit is perfect." Removing a package from his waistcoat, he opened a small box. "These diamond earrings once belonged to my grandmother. She would want you to have them as a wedding gift."

"My lord, you overwhelm me."

"Please, call me Evan. I want to remove any unnatural barriers to our relationship."

Was she dreaming? He seemed to want their marriage to be more than just an arrangement. Could it be?

"I know you are aware that I have a son. I should confess that I have not been much of a father to him. It has been just over a year since my . . . since Amelia, his mother, died. But with your help, I would like to be a better father to him."

"My . . . Evan. I had heard of your son, and I look forward to meeting him." She swallowed. She hoped she would not disappoint him as a mother to his boy. "I hope you are all right if we learn the parenting together." Her voice cracked.

"Of course, dear Charlotte." He kissed her hand. "Would you like to go to your room and freshen up? We still have time before we leave."

Fingering the ring on her left hand, she looked up at him with moisture in her eyes. "Thank you, I would."

She started to leave the room, but he held her back gently. Leaning down, he brushed his lips over hers. Then, with a little more urgency, he kissed her. She felt his tongue gently toy with her lips before she opened her mouth to him, giving him entry. Getting carried away with his kiss, she lifted her arms and placed them around his neck, absorbed in the passion.

A moment later, he broke the kiss and stepped back, breathing heavily. "I will admit to having wanted that kiss since the day you faced me in my study with your stormy green eyes demanding my apology."

"Please do not apologize for the kiss, my lord," she responded breathily. "So far, that has been the highlight of my morning."

CHAPTER NINE

I T WAS TIME to go. It pleased Evan that no setbacks had occurred—not so much because the wager he had made with Mrs. Dove-Lyon bound him to marriage; rather, he sensed a kinship with Charlotte, a bond that had formed. Perhaps it was that they were both on the brink of ruin and they were saving each other. He could not decide. However, he felt that Amelia would approve. He knew she would want him to go on and not get stuck in time. Being away from the vast amounts of alcohol and endless card games for these past two days had allowed him an opportunity to think about things.

In a little more than an hour, he would stand in front of the bishop, say wedding vows for the second time in his life, and pray this marriage would not end the same way. He would do everything in his power to make sure it did not. Edward needed a mother. Evan needed his son, and he saw that he needed a partner. He opened his bag and checked for the small wooden box of French letters he had purchased the day before. Feeling around the bottom of the bag, he felt the edge of the box. *Good, I packed them. I made a promise to myself and I would keep it.*

Banbury walked into his study. "Are you ready to leave?"

"Almost." He latched his bag, then focused on his lace cuffs, pulling them from within his overcoat sleeves. "It would disgust Charles if he saw my efforts. I imagine he is quite put out with me, wondering where I was when he would have arrived to wake me."

"Knowing Charles, he had his ear to the keyhole and already knew what was happening. I am sure the joke is on you. He is probably sleeping late this morning." Banbury howled, clapping Evan on his back. "Come. I saw Mrs. Plume heading upstairs before I came to get you. The ladies will be down in a few minutes."

"I will wake up Jason and put him in the carriage to wait." Evan pointed to his future brother-in-law, who had fallen asleep on his bed. "He should learn early that men will always have to wait on the ladies." He sniggered, carefully pulling the boy to a standing position. "It is time to go," he coaxed gently.

"Yes, my lord," Jason stood and walked with his new brother to meet his sister.

CHARLOTTE STEPPED BACK and examined herself in the full-length mirror, admiring the dark burgundy organza dress with Belgian lace overlay that Mama had just given her. Her mother had been very busy the past two days, sneaking to the seamstress and getting her to create this confection for her wedding. As much as she liked her lavender dress, this made her feel more like a woman ready to marry. Mama had gone to great lengths to both protect her and make her feel special. A small tear edged itself over the rim of her eyes and she swiped at it.

"Stand still, daughter. I would like this not to look like you tied it yourself, as did the gown this morning," her mother said with a smile in her voice. "Your father would want you to wear something that does not say mourning on your wedding day. Your uncle will get the bill in a few days." She laughed.

"Mama, he may be angry." Charlotte worried.

"I am ashamed to say that he is my brother. I am not sure what happened to him these past years. I do not recall him being so . . . so *mercenary* in his dealings with his family. I do not care if it bothers him to pay for a beautiful wedding dress for my daughter." She tightened the strings. "There! I think that looks respectable. I did not have time to get a pelisse made, however I got this beautiful muff created, and it matches the brown fur trim on the pelisse you have."

"It is almost time to go. How do I look?" Charlotte spun around slowly.

"The jewelry is lovely, darling," her mother said, kissing her head. "I have hope for you both that this will be a good union. It is Christmastide and miracles are possible with the season."

"I have heard that, Mama," she said, nibbling her bottom lip. "I barely know him, yet I feel comfortable when he is with me." Charlotte heard the hopefulness in her own voice. "He seems kind."

"His father and mother were a love match, if I recall," she mused.

"I confess, I am nervous, Mama." Charlotte had been too nervous to eat and could feel her stomach snarling in its most fervent voice.

A knock sounded on the door. "The carriage is here, my ladies," urged Mrs. Plume.

"We will be right there," Mama called out, placing the combs and her silver hand mirror back into the bag. "I think I will leave these items here and send someone for them later."

"I will ask Evan to have them brought to our townhouse." Charlotte felt the awkwardness of calling Evan's townhouse her own.

Lord Banbury rode his horse alongside their carriage to the chapel. Charlotte felt the vehicle stop and looked out the window. "There are two other carriages, Mama."

"Let me see." Her mother stretched over her and looked. "I believe that is Lord Clarendon's carriage. The other one . . ." She bit her lip. "That looks like his sister's coach. Lord and Lady Rivers." She closed the window and took a deep breath.

"I have never met them." Charlotte responded.

The door opened and Lord Banbury stood with his arm outstretched. "Clarendon is waiting in the chapel. He is already worrying over jinxing your union by seeing his bride in her finery before it is time." He shot a grin at her. "Are we ready?"

"Yes, my lord," she gave him her hand as he helped her down from the carriage. "In truth, he did not see my dress. Mama had this one made especially for today." She smiled and opened her pelisse enough for him to see the different color.

"Your mother has outdone herself. That is going to bring a smile to his lips." Banbury grinned.

I hope so. I do not think I could be more nervous. "Thank you," she answered politely.

Jason hopped out the coach. "Allow me, Mama," he said with an outstretched hand.

"Thank you, son," her mother answered, with pride in her voice and a grin stretching across her face. The two walked ahead of Charlotte and Lord Banbury.

Jason opened the door for them. Soft candlelight bathed the chapel, helped by the many intricately carved sconces that lined the walls. A candelabra with a trio of thick white candles stood in the front of the altar, which had a red velvet kneeling cushion. The cleric stood at the front, smiling and waiting for her. Lord Clarendon turned around. Seeing her, he smiled.

As Charlotte approached the front, a woman she recognized as his sister stepped into the aisle and handed her a small nosegay of greenery, white camelias and baby's breath. "Evan sent word of his nuptials and an invitation to witness. I did not think you would think of flowers but wanted to welcome you into the family," Lady Rivers smiled and squeezed her hand gently before sliding back into her seat.

"Thank you, my lady," Charlotte said, touched by her kindness.

The ceremony itself felt almost ethereal. It meant a lot that both of their families had joined them to witness their vows. As soon as the bishop pronounced them man and wife, Evan turned her face to his and kissed her lips chastely. Softly kissing her ear, he whispered, "You look very beautiful. I will delight in learning what makes you smile, my lovely countess," before turning her to face their families. "Our carriage awaits."

Mama had taken her aside to prepare her for their first night. "When he comes to you, relax and allow your body to react as it feels. Do not be ashamed of lovemaking. It is a perfectly natural act, Charlotte. Give yourself to your husband and stay true to your marriage. Be considerate and trust. Love will follow."

Wanting to know more, she had asked, "Do you truly believe I will know when and if I ever fall in love, Mama?"

Mama had squeezed her hands and kissed her on the forehead. "It is my fondest prayer for you. Trust in your heart, my daughter. You will know when it happens."

Now the time was here. As they walked past her mother and brother, Jason jumped up from the pew and hugged his sister tightly. He gazed up at her and squeezed her hand. "I shall miss you, Charlotte," he said in a small voice. The young boy glanced up at Evan with his face full of hope. "Take care of my sister, my lord."

Evan squatted down and gave the lad a hug. "I promise I will care for your sister, Jason. In fact, I hope that you and your mother to come and live with us in Epsom."

Charlotte smiled at him and leaned over to place a kiss on Jason's head. She released his hand and clasped Evan's, wiping a tear from the corner of her eye, her other hand tucked safely within his. As Evan reached for the door, the doors flew open in front of them.

"Uncle!" Charlotte gasped. "What are you doing here?" Her voice betrayed her panic.

"I should ask you that, my dear niece. What are you doing here? This"—he waved his hand toward Evan—"is *not* your betrothed." His face became mottled in anger. "How could that be? I am your guardian and I never agreed to this arrangement," he raged.

"I am not betrothed, Uncle. I am married." Charlotte squared her shoulders. "And at one and twenty years, the decision is not yours."

"And *now* she belongs to me," Evan spoke up. Charlotte's age had never entered his mind. He had not expected the baron to show up at their wedding. How did Langdale find them? Everyone had been so careful. Unwilling to believe anyone in his household would have sabotaged the day, he wondered if someone had tipped him off in the court system. Yesterday, he sent for the paperwork from the Court of Chancery necessary to move Jason's guardianship from Langdale to him once their marriage had taken place. While it probably had not been necessary, perhaps someone had asked for the details.

It mattered not. Banbury promised to ensure his barrister, Franklin, delivered it today along with proof that showed the baron was stealing the young lord's funds for his own use. The barrister had the proof and a vested interest in this family and would not let him down.

Seeing the baron edge forward, Evan stepped in front of his wife. "She is my wife, and you have no legal right to betroth her to anyone."

Seizing the opportunity, the baron grabbed his nephew's hand and began pulling him from the church. "You are leaving with me, Jason." The boy resisted, and Langdale slapped him and pulled harder.

Jason screamed and dug in his heels. "No! Charlotte! Mummy!" he cried. "I will not go with you, Uncle."

"You will not take this child," Evan seethed. He lent his considerable muscle and pulled the boy away from his uncle. "You, sir, are no gentleman," he spoke in a low tone, grabbing Langdale's arm and twisting it high behind his back.

"Ow! Let me go!" the baron screamed.

"When I do, you will have one chance to crawl back into your hole before you do something you will live to regret," he said with a dangerous edge.

"Wait!" Lady Romney pushed her way in front of the newly married couple. "This is for you, dear brother." She drew back and punched the baron in the face. Satisfied, she held her son to her side, hugging him. "Leave my son alone. What have you done to instill fear in him, Aaron? What kind of monster have you become?" Lady Romney glared at her brother.

"You punched me. You bitch!" he growled, pulling back his fist, preparing to hit Lady Romney.

Evan stepped in front of her and grabbed his arm before the baron could land a punch.

"You are not here for his welfare. You are here for his birthright," she snapped.

The baron lunged once more for the boy, and her new husband grasped his hand. "Leave here at once," Evan seethed. "I am petitioning the court for immediate guardianship of my new little brother. I suggest you leave, now!"

"You have not heard the end of this! *I am his guardian.* You had better deliver Lord Romney to my residence by three o'clock tomorrow," he shouted.

"Charlotte, take Jason to Banbury's carriage. I will meet you out there." Evan regretted the frustration in his voice. It had nothing to do with his new wife.

Banbury stepped from behind him with Lord Rivers. "We will take care of this. You and your new bride should be off." The two men secured the baron.

"We have the baron and will hold him until you and your party are safely away from here." Lord Rivers nodded toward the baron's carriage. "We will not let him go until your party is safely away."

"This will not be the last you see of me," Langdale screamed after them.

CHAPTER TEN

T HIS DAY HAD been full of surprises. Her mother had punched her uncle *in a church*.

The silence after that blow had stunned everyone, especially her uncle. Her uncle, who thought her mother had been losing her mind, had been educated by a woman mourning the loss of her husband— definitely not a muddled woman. He vowed they had not seen the last of him. Charlotte believed him.

She was married. It had happened so quickly that she lightly pinched her arm to make sure she was not asleep. No, she could definitely feel the pinch. It might even bruise, she mused, moving her hand down and touching the wedding ring she now wore, rolling it around on her finger. Evan had surprised her with his generosity and his thoughtfulness, the note, and the intimate service he had created. It was all more than she had expected, as was her husband . . . *much* more than she had expected. She glanced out the corner of her eye and caught him watching, smiling with a hint of amusement. Caught.

"Evan, thank you," she managed softly. "I could not have imagined such contentment." She wished she could say love. Perhaps that would come with time. She wanted the love match of her parents; for now, she felt contentment for the happiness on her wedding day. Without even planning it, Charlotte had had a seasonal wedding. It would have been wonderful, had her uncle not crashed the entire affair. She feared that others in attendance would recall only the last fifteen minutes.

"I consider it my duty and my pleasure to see to the happiness of my wife. It has been a while since I have said the word 'wife,' yet I find there is an easiness about it that I had not expected," he said, his eyes fixed on her.

Unexpected jealousy toward the woman who had first claimed him as husband washed over her, immediately followed by sobering guilt. Swallowing past the lump in her throat, Charlotte could only nod. Before she could utter a sound, the carriage slowed in front of his townhouse, and Evan tapped on the roof.

Charlotte glanced around however, did not see a carriage with her mother and brother. "Will Mama and Jason be following us here?" She worried her lower lip.

"Your mother felt she needed some more time to pack for their trip home. I sent two footmen to help secure the house for the evening."

"That helps, Evan," she said on a breath.

"We can retrieve them and bring them here, if you would prefer," he offered.

"I know my uncle enough to know he does not make idle threats. He acted desperate. Most of our staff have been with us for years. Mama is not afraid of my uncle; however, Jason fears him, something I failed to realize until today," she replied. "I believe they will be fine if the footmen are there to help guard the doors," she said, trying to squash the nervousness she felt. "They will be all right. I must be overreacting because of nerves."

"Should you change your mind, you have only to ask." He peeked out the window. "Our butler, Bernard, will have spotted us coming down the street. I want to give the staff a moment to assemble." His hand touched hers lightly, sending increasingly familiar jolts of sensation up her arm. "I think they are ready for us, Lady Clarendon." He turned to her and held out his hand. "Shall we?"

"Yes, my . . . Evan," she said weakly, offering him a smile.

Her husband squeezed her hand and held it softly, guiding her out of the carriage. A black oak door with a lion's head knocker opened, and a tall graying man she recognized as Bernard met them. Several house servants exited behind Bernard and lined the steps to the three-story gray stone townhouse. It was only the second time she had been here in her life, and this time, it was her home.

"Bernard, allow me to introduce you to my countess, Lady Clarendon."

"Welcome home, my lord, my lady. We have looked forward to this day, my lady," the retainer said in a voice full of sincerity.

Charlotte thought she caught a twinkle in Bernard's eye as he spoke.

Evan slid his hand down her arm to hold her hand and began introductions. "May I introduce you to Mrs. Hutchins, our housekeeper? She has been part of our family for many years."

A short woman with a gentle smile and gray hair stepped forward and stooped into a curtsy. "My lady, welcome to Clarendon House," she said genially. "We have breakfast prepared for you in the dining room."

"Thank you, Mrs. Hutchins. However, plans have changed, and it will only be Lady Clarendon and myself for now," Evan said. "We will endeavor to have a proper celebration on another day."

"Very good, my lord," the housekeeper said as she curtsied.

Evan nodded and continued with the introductions.

Having been too nervous to eat earlier, Charlotte could feel her stomach rumbling and hoped no one else could hear it. The mention of food had her stomach reacting on its own.

As they walked to the dining room, he turned to her. "If it pleases you, my dear, I would like to stay here for a few days. Not only will it allow a bit of relaxation, but I have also engaged an interior designer I would like you to meet with before travel to our country estate in Epsom. Once we arrive at Prescott Manor, we can organize our Christmastide celebration. Mrs. Hutchinson has already begun organizing items for the tenant baskets."

He nodded towards the butler. "Bernard is working with my stable hands to organize the carriages. The ride should take only a few hours." He lightly squeezed her hand. "I would like to spend our first night together alone," he finished huskily. "My sister and brother-in-law volunteered to allow Edward to stay a few more days to give us time together. I believe Edward will enjoy the time with them. They will bring Edward and Mrs. Donner, his nanny, in three days."

Charlotte was glad that he stood beside her, allowing her hair and bonnet to veil her nervous expression. As anxious as she was to meet Edward, she was nervous about becoming a wife and appreciated the extra time they would have together *alone*. As they entered the dining room, delicious smells of cooked ham, breads, and other foods wafted her way, allowing her to eat first and worry later. She would like to take a nap. However, she did not understand how to approach the topic without stirring his interest in other matters, so she decided saying nothing was perhaps best.

An hour later, they were on their way upstairs. Her stomach muscles fluttered in uneasy anticipation.

"I have had your bags delivered to your rooms, Charlotte." He opened the door to a gorgeous room bathed in warm yellow and lavender.

Unable to resist, she walked in and turned about, surveying the room. A sumptuous lavender brocade canopy cover with matching bedspread adorned an intricately carved maple bed. Lush patterned carpet surrounded the bed on all sides, reaching to all four walls. A coordinated dressing table and wardrobe completed the larger furnishings, while a plush lavender Chippendale chair sat near the fireplace. Pale yellow velour drapes with light lavender cording showed off large hand-blown double-paned windows that looked outside upon a garden. "What a beautiful room," she enthused.

"I hoped you would like it, however you have leave to decorate it in any colors or fabrics you so desire." He gazed at her.

"And where are your accommodations, my lord?" she asked coyly. He gave her a look that made her body quiver. *I am married to him*, she reminded herself.

"Glad you asked," he said, taking her hand and leading her through a door that blended in with the wallpaper next to her wardrobe. They walked through a short corridor linking the suites into a room decorated in deep greens and dark wood.

The smell of sandalwood lingered in the air near his bed, and a fire roared in the fireplace. Two mahogany chairs sat with a small table between them about six feet from the fireplace. It was enough to keep the occupants comfortable without making them too hot.

"I thought we could have our dinner up here tonight," he said as a look of emotion she could not identify passed over his face. He replaced it with a smile.

"I would like that, Evan."

EVAN WATCHED HIS wife's face. She was lovely, almost perfection when she flashed her emerald green eyes in fits of pique. That had been his first vision of her—her eyes sparking and temper riled.

He had wanted to welcome Charlotte to her new home a little more smoothly. But the baron's ill-timed intrusion threw those plans into disarray, similar to the timing of her intrusion—and he used that word loosely—into his life. Charlotte had intruded—or rather burst in upon his solace with her anger and indignance at his behavior, heralding attention to his conduct. There was so much more to her— something that made him want to help her, and not just because it would help him. He *meant* his vows—those that promised to be loyal, generous, and provide protection. He would welcome her to his life, his home, and with care, to his bed. He needed to be careful that what happened to Amelia would never happen to Charlotte. His son needed a mother. And he could not lose another wife.

Charlotte's earlier tensions over her mother and brother seemed to have eased, however his had not. Someone had tipped off Langdale, but who? Should he send for her family? Charlotte had seemed satisfied that the footmen could provide the security needed. Why, then, was his gut telling him something different? "My dear, please allow me to pen a note to Banbury. I have a favor to ask."

"Of course," she said absently.

"Have a seat by the fire and warm yourself. I shall return in about ten minutes."

Charlotte nodded and sat in a leather armchair to the left of his fireplace. He took an extra moment and pulled up the small matching ottoman and lifted her feet onto it before leaving the room.

"I will not be long, dear," he said, taking a quick backward glance before leaving the room.

Evan hurried downstairs and extracted a sheet of vellum from the box on his desk. Quickly, he penned Banbury a note asking his friend if he would visit his mother-in-law and convince them to stay with him. Knowing Banbury, he would do it without being asked, however just the same, he would feel better knowing his new family was safe. Langdale had acted almost rabid earlier.

Evan pulled out a burgundy taper and heated it, allowing it to drip on the outside of his folded note. Using his signet ring, he sealed it.

Ringing for his butler, he eased back in his chair and waited. Bernard responded in a thrice. "Bernard, please have this delivered immediately to Lord Banbury. Have the messenger wait to get a response."

"Right away, my lord."

"One more thing. Remind Charles he has the night off but ask him to be ready to leave three days hence with the rest of the estate staff to move to Epsom."

"Right away, my lord. I believe your valet is in the kitchen eating a noon meal. I shall apprise him of your instructions."

"Excellent. And please let me know when you have a reply from Lord Banbury."

His retainer nodded and left to dispatch his note. Feeling somewhat better, Evan headed back upstairs to his room.

The sight that greeted him there stirred his loins. His wife was curled up in his chair, asleep in front of the fireplace. He pulled the drapes and turned down the light in the room. Walking to his bride, he lifted her and moved her to his bed, pulling back the coverlet with one hand while holding her with the other. Satisfied that she was comfortable, he sat in the chair she had just vacated and pulled off his boots. Luckily, these were looser than others and slid off easily. Taking off his waistcoat, he untied his cravat, opened the neck of his shirt, and slid under the covers next to her.

The fresh scent of jasmine stirred his need. Gently, he lifted her hand and with his thumb, rubbed the inside of her hand in little circles. Her eyes fluttered open, and a lazy smile creased her face as she turned to him.

"Shall I stop?" he asked, his voice husky.

Charlotte closed her eyes. "No . . . Evan." A smile lifted her lips.

Evan leaned down and gently brushed her mouth. With more force, he kissed her, his teeth nibbling gently on her lip. Gentle coaxing from his tongue gained him entry, and she pulled back her neck to give more room.

"Evan . . . we are in your bed . . ." the words fell away as his breath heated her neck.

"And? It is our wedding day. I pulled the curtains. The day and the night are ours to spend at our leisure—until we are persuaded by hunger to gain sustenance. What better way could there be to spend our time?" His breath fanned her ears.

Tenderly, he slipped her sleeves from her arms, exposing her breast. "Allow me to warm you, wife."

"Evan," she murmured, wrapping her hands around his neck and pulling him closer.

Evan reveled in the contrasting feeling of her heated hands touching the cool skin of his neck. His head dipped, and with his teeth, he pulled the shoulders of her gown away from her, freeing both breasts. Charlotte moved her head back and gave a guttural hum as he gently pulled one breast into his mouth, licking and suckling before moving to the next one to give equal measure. Lifting his head, he moved back to her mouth, kissing her and nibbling her lower lip slowly as his hand moved under her dress to her moist folds. "I want you," he whispered against the lobes of her ear, sending tingles across her shoulders and into the base of her skull.

NEVER HAD SHE experienced such delicious feelings. "Evan . . . do not stop . . . I want . . . I need . . ." She panted, unable to comprehend what she wanted. All she knew was the overpowering feeling of desire. Pulling his head back to her breasts, she reveled in the warm wetness of his mouth. She could feel her nipples pebbling beneath his touch. "I have never felt this hot tingling in my . . . my insides," she gasped, unable to think of another word yet needing to tell him, hoping he would understand.

"I want to please you before we couple," he breathed in her ear as his fingers teased her folds. "My need is almost unbearable," he whispered and adjusted himself over her, probing her moist core.

Charlotte gasped as her center convulsed from his ministrations. Tender lips covered hers and their tongues touched, danced, and swirled against the insides of their mouths between heated breaths. She squeezed her eyes closed, hoping to hold onto the sensation of floating above her body.

"I think you are ready . . ." he said between pants, reaching down and opening his placket, then kicking off his breeches and smalls. He adjusted himself over her. "My darling, I will take my time. You will feel a slight pain, although I promise it will get better," he exhaled, his words coming between heated breaths.

"Yes . . ." she said on a sigh, unsure of what pain he spoke. She had only experienced pleasure with his attentions.

Evan moved to her entry, and she felt a piercing pain that lasted for a moment. Her husband stopped. She struggled to get her breath before he began once more, moving slowly, inciting her own body to respond to each of his movements. At the pinnacle, when she felt her body would explode, he withdrew, pulling back away from her. Too inexperienced to say anything, she lay there, feeling cheated yet not understanding why. She was afraid to speak. Long moments passed before finally, she summoned her courage and rose, her arms steadying her as she pushed herself up to a sitting position. "What just happened?" she asked. "Why did you pull away? Did I do something wrong?" She swiped at a rogue tear that appeared at the corner of her face.

He lay next to her, his eyes on the ceiling, staring. His breaths slowed until finally, he spoke. "No, Charlotte. It was my fear that forced me back from you. I want you, and I know she would want me happy," he spoke the words in a low, pained voice.

"She? Your first wife?" Charlotte spoke cautiously, suddenly terrified and unsure of why.

"It is not fair to you, however I cannot risk losing you the way I lost her," he choked.

"Look at me," she pleaded softly. She waited. Long minutes passed before he rolled to her. "Evan, I do not know what our future will be, yet I cannot allow fear ruling our present. If we do, surely much of the best part of lives will pass us by, unlived and unknown."

He stared at her eyes as his own watered. "I never wanted to marry again," he said, pausing.

Her breathing went still. What was he saying?

"Then you happened, and I gave into my need for a wife, a mother for my child, a companion . . ."

She leaned up on her elbow and placed a finger over his lips, gently stopping him. Suddenly, she understood. "Evan, I will be all of those, and childbirth is dangerous. While I cannot promise you not to leave you in death, I can promise that I will fight for our life together." She tried to keep her tears at bay and her voice steady.

He rose over her, staring into her green eyes. "Charlotte," he choked and lowered himself to kiss her, adjusting himself into her once more. "Give me time. While we have not known each other long, I feel that I know your heart. And I need to share mine. I pledge to do my best by you." He leaned in and kissed her tenderly. "Tonight has so much more promise."

CHAPTER ELEVEN

E VAN AWOKE HOURS later. There was a noise downstairs. *Come to think of it, I have not heard from Banbury.* After making love with his wife twice, they fell asleep in each other's arms, no longer able to ignore that need. Reaching over, he opened a small drawer to his nightstand. The French letters he purchased were still there. He had forgotten to use them, although he had withdrawn each time before spilling his seed. Evan glanced over at his still sleeping wife and a small pain of guilt stung his heart as he remembered her words. *She would fight for their life together.* He found Charlotte to be a good listener and talking last night, even in the heat of making love, had made a difference. He would try harder. Perhaps discussing it was the key to moving past it.

Quietly, he slid to the side of the bed and put on his breeches. Then, slipping into his green velvet robe, he secured it with a sash. Male voices sounded from below; however, he could not make out what was being said. When he reached the top of the stairs, he saw Bernard addressing a messenger who stood ready to leave. The man wore regimentals and appeared confused.

"Good sir, Lord and Lady Clarendon are not available. Can you leave a message for his lordship?"

"I was told by Lady Romney that this was an important message and to see that they received it as soon as possible," the messenger responded, frustrated with Bernard's casual dismissal.

"Who wishes to see us, Bernard?" Evan asked as he hastened down the stairs.

The retainer turned. "My lord, this gentleman wishes to speak with you and Lady Clarendon."

"Thank you, Bernard. I will see him in my study." Who would come to see him in regimentals?

The door to the study closed, and the boyish man walked to the desk and held out a missive to him.

"I heard you mention Lady Romney's name," Evan prodded gently, opening and attempting to scan the document.

"Yes, my lord. I know of no other way to say this other than the message upset Lady Romney when she read it and asked that I deliver it to you immediately. Under the circumstances, I thought it best. It is news of her son," he finished politely.

"I am Lady Romney's son-in-law. My wife is resting. This is about Matthew?" Evan held his breath as he focused again on the document. "It says he is no longer presumed dead," he said, hoping he had read it correctly. "Where is he?"

"We do not know exactly," the courier hesitated before continuing. "I will tell you all I have been told on the matter. We know Colonel Romney had been badly injured and a local woman found him sometime after the battle and took him home with her to try and nurse him to back to health. This information was discovered by a small contingent of Major General Lambert's men sent to locate the bodies of our fallen officers. Oddly, they received word of a woman that had taken two injured men into her home, hoping to help them. They passed the information on to Major General Lambert who later, sent more men to track her down. One of the men was confirmed to be Colonel Romney. However, the colonel had improved and had left two days ahead of our men's arrival, telling her it was dangerous to her for him to stay. She believes he headed home."

"Did he board a ship? How long has the Crown known of this? And why are we just hearing of it? His late father died thinking his son had passed," Evan said through clenched teeth, realizing this man was not responsible for the message, only its delivery. "His father hired an investigator," he softened his tone and kept reading.

Matthew had sustained a head injury—probably the reason they failed to account for him after the battle. "Thank you." Evan decided that the messenger needed no further information and had gone beyond his normal job. He fished a coin from his drawer and passed it to him. "My wife and I appreciate your thoughtfulness, and most especially the news." He closed up the missive. "I assume we will hear of any updates on Colonel Romney," he said, looking up from the paper.

"Yes, my lord."

He walked the courier to the door. When he closed it behind him, he called to Bernard.

"Yes, my lord?" Bernard came from around the corner.

Had Bernard waited there the whole time he had spoken to the courier? The more he thought about it, the funnier he thought it to be. *That's how the old codger knows everything.* He smiled to himself. "Have you received a message for me from Lord Banbury?"

"Yes, my lord." He picked up the salver and moved it in Evan's direction. "It came not long after you posted your own."

Evan opened Banbury's message and scanned it quickly. His friend had gone to Charlotte's home and would stay there to watch over the place. He imagined that Lady Romney would have told him about Matthew, so he would wait on that until tomorrow. Perhaps there would be more news, he thought, making his way upstairs, thinking to wake Charlotte with the update on her brother. He was almost to the top when pounding sounded on the front door.

"My lord, I will see to it. I do not recall a time with more traffic . . ." Bernard said as he opened the door.

Banbury stood there for a second before pushing past. "I hoped that you and Lady Clarendon were together. Is she alone upstairs?"

"Yes, in my bed," Evan supplied. "I had a courier. What is this about?"

"Her younger brother is missing. I believe they are both in danger."

Evan took the stairs two at a time with Banbury in tow.

"She is in danger," Banbury half-shouted.

"Danger? What are you about?" Evan asked, opening the door to his room. The window was open and his bed was empty. His heart hit the floor.

Evan ran to the bed. Her clothes and shoes were gone. Could she have gotten dressed before she left? A small cloth lay beside the bed. He picked it up and sniffed. Ether.

Every scenario led him to a dark answer he could not accept. Frustrated, he sat down on the edge of the bed he had shared with his wife less than an hour before and dropped his head in his hands.

"Get yourself together, man!" Banbury touched him lightly on the shoulders. "We must leave immediately. I received a message from Titan at Mrs. Dove-Lyon's. He wanted us to know Lord Langdale had put the word out that he was hiring today. And worse, he planted a mole in the Romney household," Banbury added.

"Her servants have been there for years, according to Charlotte." He grew quiet. "All except for her lady's maid, Jane."

"I hired a Bow Street Runner when I heard from Titus, not wanting to bother you with this and hoping it was much ado about nothing. I am hoping he was watching the house and has followed the young lord. Her uncle is desperate, mad, or both. I have a grim feeling." Banbury was direct.

"We should go to the Romney home and question Jane. She has to know something." Evan was feeling desperate himself. He pulled on his boots, shirt, and waistcoat, and the two men sprinted down the stairs. "Have my horse—"

Banbury interrupted him. "Your horse is outside. I asked the stable hand to get him ready when I arrived."

Ten minutes later, they arrived at the Romney house. Evan did not envy Lady Romney. She had lost her husband, thought her eldest son had died in a strange land, was trying to cope with the abduction of her young son, and in a moment, would find out her daughter was also missing.

He pounded on the door until Myers opened it. "My lord, Lady Romney is in her parlor. She is beside herself. Another gentleman and a lady, a Mrs. Dove-Lyon and Mr. Titan, arrived and are with her," Myers said as succinctly as he could with the household staff running all around them.

"Myers, locate Jane and bring her to us."

"Yes, my lord." He nodded at Mrs. Graves, who turned and flew up the stairs to the servants' quarters.

Both men paused, fortifying before opening the parlor door.

The sight of Mrs. Dove-Lyon in the room with his mother-in-law should have shocked him, yet Evan said nothing. There were rumors that the Widow had a heart. Perhaps the rumors were true because there she sat, comforting Lady Romney. She stood and motioned for the two men to follow her to the other side of the room.

"Several of my men are on the dock looking for a specific boat, a boat that heads to the Orient when it leaves this dock. It is my belief that Lord Langdale"—she practically spit the name—"has ordered his niece and nephew taken aboard." She did not mince words. "Lord Langdale used Jane, the new maid, to monitor his niece."

"How do you know all of this?" Evan challenged. She alluded to slave trading. It had been outlawed several years back. However, there had been renewed suspicion that it still operated illicitly.

Mrs. Dove-Lyon drew up her shoulders. "I understand you are quite distressed but know that I am here to help. There are two boats due to leave port tonight, according to the information Titan secured. He will go with you. You must hurry."

Being told what to do by this woman rankled him, but he quickly set it aside. She had forced him into a marriage, and while he had satisfied that debt, he would owe one of gratitude if they could save his wife in time.

Screaming in the hall alerted him to Jane. "In here, missy." The housekeeper opened the door and thrust the girl inside. "I caught her in Lady Clarendon's room going through her drawers." Mrs. Graves held up a small velvet bag, which he assumed contained some of Charlotte's jewelry. "I will put these away."

"Thank you, Mrs. Graves." Evan stood in front of the maid. "My wife has been taken. Tell me what you know. My wife's life could be in peril," he said as forcefully as possible.

"He will kill me," she cried, collapsing to the floor.

"Who? Who will kill you?" Banbury asked, pulling her to her feet.

"Lord Langdale. He threatened to if I let anyone know he had hired me."

"Well, you will be lucky to live a month in Newgate if you do not tell me what I am asking. You have taken part in the abduction of two peers of the realm."

"I heard him mention a ship named *The Mermaid*," the young woman cried.

"I saw that ship," Titus spoke up.

"Where is Langdale?" Evan demanded of Jane.

"I do not know—in his home, maybe, waiting to hear," she cried.

"I will take two footmen and go to Langdale's," Banbury said. "You and Titan go to *The Mermaid*. As soon as I have Langdale in the magistrate's hands, we will follow."

"Thank you, Christopher," Evan said quietly.

Myers stepped in. "I will handle the situation here." He snapped his fingers, and a footman materialized from behind him. "Take her to Lady Clarendon's wardrobe and lock her inside," he demanded. "Make sure her mouth is muffled and her hands are tied."

"Yes, sir." The footman did as asked.

"Hurry, gentlemen," Mrs. Dove-Lyon pleaded. *The Mermaid* sails tonight."

The four men took off out the door. The footman and Banbury left for Langdale's. Titan and Evan mounted their horses and went in the opposite direction, heading to the shipyards of the East End.

"If you do not mind, my lord," the bouncer began, "I know this area. Follow my lead, and I believe we will have a better chance of finding the young lord and your wife."

Evan nodded as a new realization soured his stomach. Titan was right. All this time he had worried about losing a wife to childbirth when greater dangers existed. Charlotte had been right, and he would tell her. Life was to be lived.

The dock area was black, and the air was thick with the smells of urine and vomit. Evan tried to keep his head down, hoping to evade the odors. The two men slowed their horses and rode slowly and deliberately down a cobblestone street that ran alongside a large corner tavern known as the Lion's Head. "We will pay someone in the stable near the pub to hold our horses, my lord. From there, we will not be far from *The Mermaid*."

Just as Titan had said, he rode to the stable at the back of the pub and whistled. A young street urchin came forth. "Watch these horses. Do not take your eyes away."

"Aye, guv." The child smiled with several teeth missing. Titan tossed him a shilling, which he promptly bit before putting it into his pocket. Evan handed over his horse and also gave him a shilling.

"We don't have far, my lord." Titan pointed to the area beyond a row of buildings. A group of men dressed in sailors' garb stumbled by, singing and laughing. Titan motioned to keep to the shadows of the building, allowing the men to pass without noticing them. Evan wished he had worn his greatcoat and a sword. All he had was a small knife in his saddlebag. The closer he got to the water, the colder he became.

The two men made it past the next row of businesses and buildings, bringing the ships into view. One ship had a lot of activity around it on the docks. *The Mermaid.* They edged closer and heard voices.

"Aye, the baron said he'd be here with money before the ship sailed. I want more. These two are worth more than we asked," the larger man said, slapping an enormous arm on the barrel behind him.

"He's late!" a smaller man said. "The damn little lord bit me, so I hit 'im! The baron won't know it where they're going."

"The frilly piece was a bright and breezy take and was nearly wearing nothing. Took my pleasure with dressing her, I did, until she woke up like some sort of vicious animal. Gave me a black eye, she did," the larger man said, touching a swollen eye.

Titan picked up two large sticks that were laying nearby and tossed one to Evan, signaling to continue in the shadows and move behind the two of them. They slipped behind the barrels.

A shriek sounded from the barrel behind the larger man, and he slammed his fist into it. "Shut up, woman! You'll be lucky ta make the ship alive."

Evan's temper flared. Not waiting a moment longer, he took the stick and slammed it into the man's head from behind. Titus did the same, wincing as the smaller man crumpled into a heap at their feet.

The two men pried open the barrels and sighed in relief.

"Are you well, my dear?" Evan's voice was low. His wife sat huddled in the barrel. Her dress was torn but covered most of her.

"Yes. Aside from my pride, I am fine. My uncle paid them to hie us off to the ship. They called it slavery. I did not know such a ship existed. I was afraid I would never see you again." Her voice trembled, but she did not cry.

Evan helped her from the barrel and gave her a brief kiss. "Stay in the shadow. We will be back." Evan pulled his waistcoat off and handed it to Charlotte. She hugged her brother close, and the two of them did as he bid, staying in the shadows. Aside from a few bruises and being bound and gagged, Charlotte and Jason were mostly uninjured. He was grateful.

A whistle from the ship signaled that it was nearly ready to pull out. Evan and Titan worked quickly and stuffed the two unconscious men into the barrels that Charlotte and Jason had vacated, securing the lids.

Keeping their heads down, they rolled the two barrels to the edge of the dock near the boat's gangplank. Two sailors in striped uniforms came down, accepted the barrels, and rolled them to the ship and up the gangway, closing the gate behind them.

THE FOUR OF them made it back to the Romney house without further incident, where they met up with Banbury, who appeared to be leaving. They had convinced Lady Romney that lying down could do her some good, and she was sound asleep on the settee. Mrs. Graves nudged her mistress when they brought her son into the room.

"Mama!" he ran to her, and she pulled him close.

"My darlings!" The woman hugged and kissed Charlotte before snatching up her son and smothering him in kisses and hugs. Charlotte turned and threw her arms around her mother and her brother.

The scene tugged at Evan's heart, when he realized that he had never shown his own son this much affection. *I will remedy that soon.* He cleared his throat. "What about Langdale?"

"We secured him quickly and turned him over to the magistrate, who said he will investigate immediately. I instructed the Bow Street Runner to assist him," Banbury replied. "I will also send a note to the regent and ask him to help us sort this situation. It deserves his attention."

"I will add to that note, if you do not mind," Evan added. "I believe an audit of the funds Langdale handled would be in order."

"What did you do with the men that had taken Charlotte and the young lord?" Banbury asked.

Titan tipped his hat, smiling mischievously. "This is our cue to leave, Mrs. Dove-Lyon. I should get you back," he said, grinning toward his mysterious employer.

"Wait. I want to know what you did with the men too," she said. Evan could not be sure, but he thought he saw the red lips spread into an enormous smile beneath the black veil.

"Madam, you would approve." The sizeable man laughed. "I hope seasickness plagues neither of the men, because they are on their way to the Orient in the same barrels they used for her ladyship and his lordship."

"Well, now." She clapped softly. "This is a perfect outcome. Now, I must get back to my business." She turned to Lady Romney. "I do not have many friends in this world, but I hope I can count you as one, as I have always counted your departed husband. Call upon me if ever I can help you."

"Thank you, my dear," Lady Romney said as she gave the Widow a hug.

Evan stepped forward. "Mrs. Dove-Lyon, I am once again in your debt," he said earnestly.

"Lord Clarendon, there is no debt, so long as you give this lovely lady your devotion and your loyalty," she said with her voice full of gaiety.

Evan hugged his wife close. Uncaring that her dress was damaged and dirty, he tipped her head up and kissed her.

EPILOGUE

Epsom, Surrey
Christmas Eve, 1816

SITTING IN THE freshly painted white rocking chair, Charlotte leaned back and rocked their very engaging young son, Edward. She felt well rested for the first time in more than weeks, since having thrust herself into the life of the man whose carriage had nearly run over her younger brother, Jason. Two weeks felt like a lifetime. Today, she only wanted to revel in her life, their son, this beautiful home, and the adoration of her husband.

The robin's egg walls and cheerful yellow gingham curtains had given new life to the nursery her husband had known as a child. Mrs. Donner was a jewel and forever her employer's supporter, having been given leave to decorate her worksite as she pleased. Earlier that week, she and the nanny had hired a seamstress to make curtains and matching lavender bedding for the woman's bedroom, which adjoined the nursery.

Since meeting him two weeks past, she had spent every spare moment getting to know this dear sweet boy and falling in love with him over and over. Whenever he smiled up at her with those crystal blue eyes and pink cherub cheeks, her heart melted.

Evan was getting used to fatherhood, and she was enjoying being a mother, although she hoped that one day she and Evan would add to the nursery. Mrs. Donner kept Edward to a regimen, but Charlotte believed parents should also be engaged and encouraged her husband to join her in the nursery whenever possible. Her parents had stayed involved with her and her siblings and considered their nanny part of the family.

Tomorrow would be Christmas, and Mrs. Donner was downstairs with their housekeeper making sure that all the boxes were ready for delivery to the tenants. Charlotte planned to accompany Evan and deliver each one, meeting each of the people whose work supported their home. Her father had always said that the token of appreciation could bridge immeasurable chasms. Charlotte saw it as her job to keep Evan's tenants engaged and feeling valued in their lives.

"Ma-ma!" Edward played with her hair, pulling it loose around the edges while flashing the infectious grin of his. Charlotte felt at peace and hoped Amelia would approve of her love for Edward.

"Are you ready for your nap story?" She kissed his nose and giggled.

"Da-da!" He said proudly, pointing behind her.

Before Charlotte could turn, she felt a warm kiss on her neck. Her husband had been a complete surprise. While neither had mentioned love, their actions told her much. Making love had been more complete ever since she had been rescued from the dockside. There were no guarantees in life, yet they had decided that together they would take that chance and welcome the wonderful promises that life together could offer them.

"We have visitors downstairs who would like to see you . . ."

"Mama and Jason have arrived!" she exclaimed. Giving the cherub on her lap a quick peck, she bounced up from the chair. Her mother and brother had decided to join them on Christmas Eve, giving the three of them time as a family to adjust. It also allowed Mama to properly pack her things before joining them in the country. This would be her first Christmas without Father.

"Ahem!" The feminine voice came from the doorway behind Evan. Both Charlotte and Evan turned as one.

"May I meet my new daughter and see my grandson?" A female voice sounded as blue satin skirts whooshed from behind Evan and came forward.

"Mother! This is a grand surprise," Evan gave his mother a kiss on the cheek. "We had not expected you back from Italy this soon. Let me introduce you to my countess."

"Please." She tapped her son gently on the arm. "No need for formalities with me, my son. I am thrilled to meet your new wife. I arrived after Lady Romney and did not want to make a fuss." Turning to her son's wife, she added, "Charlotte, you will find me unconventional at times. It happens mostly when I am overly excited," the dowager countess said, smiling. She pulled a brown wrapped package from behind her. "This is a small painting that I had framed for the nursery," she said, passing the gift to Charlotte. "I hope it resembles Edward," she laughed. "I have been away for what seems like forever, even though it was just two months. So much has happened!"

"Thank you. This is so unexpected," responded Charlotte. She unwrapped the gift to reveal a little boy sitting on his father's lap, enjoying a book. "We shall install it above this rocking chair. It is perfect! Evan sits down each night and reads Edward a story. You have quite captured it without even being here."

"I am so pleased," the dowager said as she wiped the corner of her eye. "My heart is full of joy for all of you, most especially my grandson."

"We should retire to the parlor where your mother and Jason are waiting. I have news of Matthew but would like to share it with everyone," Evan spoke, his voice full of happiness.

"I will join the others in the parlor and give you two a few minutes together before you come down," his mother offered.

"Your mother is very intuitive," Charlotte whispered as the woman left the room. "I was just wishing to have a moment to kiss you," she added, leaning up and brushing his lips.

"Mmm, yes. Mother reads people better than most, I think," he said, leaning in to deepen the kiss, then trailed small kisses on her neck.

"Tell me. I am anxious to hear," she laughed. "You mentioned Matthew."

"Ah, yes. Matt. I almost forgot. Wife, you stir my blood in ways I cannot adequately describe," he whispered huskily. He held up the letter. "Matthew is presumed well. He seems to be headed slowly north toward Boston or New York, most likely in hopes of finding a ship home."

"Mama will be so relieved. She has been heartsick over all that has happened. I have worried so much for her."

"The man your father hired to find Matthew sent this information to both the Crown and to your mother." He continued, "With the arrest of Langdale, the man I hired to find Matthew forwarded this news to me, thinking Langdale had probably intercepted the original message meant for your family.

"I look forward to seeing your brother home," Evan added. "We had many good times at school and while the age of our boyhood shenanigans has long passed, the bonds we forged have not."

"I should like to know more about this side of you, dear husband." Charlotte gave a sly look at Evan. "I reread all of Matthew's letters he sent me while at Eton and felt there was a good bit of mischief attached to your education." She held her hands over Edward's ears. "Let us not create a child bursting to partake of such tomfoolery," she said good-naturedly. "'Twill give my heart a start, to be sure!"

"I also have news of *Uncle Langdale*," Evan added, emphasizing the name. "It is only a small update. The Prince Regent has taken a personal interest in the case and had Langdale moved to the Tower. Additionally, an agent of the Crown is working with your father's lawyer to determine how much damage Langdale did to your brother's estate and what measures can be taken to reverse some of the damage. However, there are no certainties."

"That's still promising news, Evan. I hope to have seen the last of Uncle," Charlotte said with a grimace. His mother's visit and the news that Matthew was well were joyous surprises. Charlotte hoped that what she was about to tell Evan would be just as welcome. Placing his hand on her stomach, she raised her eyes to his face.

"I may have an early autumn present for you, dearest husband," she said, color deepening in her face. "I should wait longer before saying something, but I find I am not able."

A shocked look passed over his face that frightened her.

"You think you could be pregnant . . . this soon?" he enquired, a smile thinning his lips.

"I have missed my courses, and they have never been late before. I am hoping that they will not come," she explained quietly, trying to read his face.

Evan glanced down at Edward's blond curls and blue eyes looking up at him while he squeezed his wife's finger. He pulled her close and cradled her face in his hands, kissing her on the nose. "I am afraid but no longer paralyzed by my fear. You have taught me to love and trust. I love you, my darling Charlotte. You will be a wonderful mother to this baby as you already are to our dear Edward."

"You mean that? You *love* me?" she asked with tears glistening in her eyes.

He leaned in and kissed her deeply. "I do, so help me . . . I have fallen madly in love with you, my beautiful Lyon's Prey."

At the reference to Mrs. Dove-Lyon and the lost bet, Charlotte smiled. "I love you too, Evan, and I will do my best to never make you sorry you lost that bet."

About the Author

Anna St. Claire is a big believer that *nothing* is impossible if you believe in yourself. She sprinkles her stories with laughter, romance, mystery and lots of possibilities, adhering to the belief that goodness and love will win the day.

Anna is both an avid reader author of American and British historical romance. She and her husband live in Charlotte, North Carolina with their two dogs and often, their two beautiful granddaughters, who live nearby. *Daughter, sister, wife, mother, and Mimi*—all life roles that Anna St. Claire relishes and feels blessed to still enjoy. And she loves her pets – dogs and cats alike, and often inserts them into her books as secondary characters. And she loves chocolate and popcorn, a definite nod to her need for sweet followed by salty...*but not together*— a tasty weakness!

Anna relocated from New York to the Carolinas as a child. Her mother, a retired English and History teacher, always encouraged Anna's interest in writing, after discovering short stories she would write in her spare time.

As a child, she loved mysteries and checked out every *Encyclopedia Brown* story that came into the school library. Before too long, her fascination with history and reading led her to her first historical romance—Margaret Mitchell's *Gone With The Wind*, now a treasured, but weathered book from being read multiple times. The day she discovered Kathleen Woodiwiss,' books, *Shanna* and *Ashes In The Wind*, Anna became hooked. She read every historical romance that came her way and dreams of writing her own historical romances took seed.

Today, her focus is primarily the Regency and Civil War eras, although Anna enjoys almost any period in American and British history. She would love to connect with any of her readers on her website – www.annastclaire.com, through email – annastclaireauthor @gmail.com, Instagram – annastclaire_author, BookBub – bookbub. com/profile/anna-st-claire, Twitter – @1AnnaStClaire, Facebook – facebook.com/authorannastclaire or on Amazon – amazon.com/ Anna-St-Claire/e/B078WMRHHF.

Made in United States
Troutdale, OR
07/10/2024

21153460R00066